SMOKIES SPECIAL AGENT

LENA DIAZ

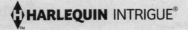

HARLEQUIN INTRIGUE®

Thank you Allison Lyons and Nalini Akolekar. As always, thank you Connie Mann and Jan Jackson for your friendship and support in this crazy business.

ISBN-13: 978-1-335-60434-7

Smokies Special Agent

Recycling programs for this product may not exist in your area.

Copyright © 2019 by Lena Diaz

HARLEQUIN®
www.Harlequin.com

Printed in U.S.A.

Lena Diaz was born in Kentucky and has also lived in California, Louisiana and Florida, where she now resides with her husband and two children. Before becoming a romantic suspense author, she was a computer programmer. A Romance Writers of America Golden Heart® Award finalist, she has also won the prestigious Daphne du Maurier Award for Excellence in Mystery/Suspense. To get the latest news about Lena, please visit her website, lenadiaz.com.

Visit the Author Profile page at Harlequin.com.

CAST OF CHARACTERS

Duncan McKenzie—As a special agent with the National Park Service, he's tasked with finding out why women are disappearing in the Great Smoky Mountains.

Remi Jordan—This Colorado native will do anything, even risk her career with the FBI, to prove there's a serial killer stalking women in national parks.

Oliver "Pop" McAlister—The most senior ranger working in the Great Smoky Mountains, he might have the critical piece of the puzzle to solve Remi's sister's disappearance.

Yeong Lee—Duncan's boss at the NPS assigns him to keep an eye on Special Agent Remi Jordan and find out what secrets she's hiding from both of them.

Leon Johnson—Remi's boss at the FBI denounces her far-fetched theories about a serial killer stalking national parks, forcing her to risk her career to discover the truth.

Kurt Vale—While hiking the Appalachian Trail, he's nearly killed by Special Agent Remi Jordan when she thinks he has a gun. Was Remi mistaken? Or is Vale more than just a hiker?

Billy Hendricks—After being rejected by Remi's sister, did he exact his revenge by kidnapping and possibly killing her? Or was his obsession with her just a misunderstanding?

Chapter One

Frozen ground crunched behind her. Remi Jordan whirled around. The trail was empty. She whipped back the other way. Nothing except shadows met her searching gaze. The woods had gone as silent as a tomb. Even the icy wind had quit blowing, as if the entire mountain was holding its breath, waiting to see what would happen next.

Waiting to see if *she* would be next?

Remi drew a slow, deep breath, the chilly air prickling her lungs. Sound could carry for miles up here, or not at all, and seemed to bounce all over the place. Figuring out the direction it came from was nearly impossible. Someone was definitely stalking her. But figuring out where they were, and how far away, was beginning to feel like an impossibility.

Stepping to the side of the path, she listened intently and pretended to study the two-by-six white blaze painted on the bark of a spruce tree. Similar patches of paint in varying colors served as guideposts all up and down the Appalachian Trail. She'd seen dozens of them since she'd begun her daily AT hikes on the Tennessee side of the Great Smoky Mountains National Park.

She shoved both her hands into her jacket pockets. If the person following her was close enough to see her, he probably thought she looked vulnerable, oblivious to danger. But she was far from helpless. Her right hand caressed the butt of a loaded SIG Sauer 9 mm hidden in her pocket.

The gun had been a gift from her father on her eighteenth birthday, the butt of the weapon engraved with her name. He'd been critically ill for months and knew he wouldn't make it to her nineteenth. It was his fervent hope that the pistol would do what he no longer could—protect her, keep his remaining daughter safe.

Her throat tightened. If her father knew what she was doing, he'd feel hurt, betrayed. He'd berate her for taking unnecessary risks with her safety. But how could she sit and do nothing? Ten years ago she'd done nothing. Then her twin sister had disappeared and was never seen again. That one, horrible mistake haunted her every single day. Having another woman's death on her bruised and battered conscience was more than she could bear.

As if a switch had been flipped, the wind picked up again. The crisp pine-scented air was heavy with the promise of snow as it whipped the long blond strands of her hair back from her face. Evergreen branches clacked together, their needles brushing against bark with an unsettling *shuh-shuh* sound. And somewhere overhead a bird twittered, as if everything was right with the world. As if nature itself denied the evil that had once taken place here, evil that was again poised to strike, to destroy another family, unless Remi could find a way to stop it.

Could she have imagined footfalls echoing her own? Could she be wrong in thinking that someone had been trying to match his steps to hers, to disguise his pursuit? She considered the idea, then discarded it. Her faults were many, but *imagining* things wasn't one of them. There was no other reasonable explanation for the sounds she'd been hearing since starting out on this trail at sunup.

I'm close this time, Becca. So close. I can feel it.

She could almost see her stargazing, unicorn-loving twin sister rolling her eyes in reply. It was her signature trademark, especially when the two of them were together. When they were kids, it had made Remi furious. Now, she wished with all her heart that she could see her sister roll her eyes at her just one more time.

I miss you so much, Becca. So. Much.

Once again, she started down the well-worn path. It wasn't long before another sound sent a fresh rush of goose bumps across her skin. This time, she didn't stop. Instead, she scanned the woods from beneath her lashes, trying not to be too obvious as she searched the shadows surrounding her.

What had she heard? The whisper of fabric against a tree? A rattle of loose rocks across a part of the path sheltered by the tree canopy, where there wasn't much snow to reveal anyone's passage? Or was it simply a raccoon skittering through the underbrush searching for its next meal?

This feeling of unease outdoors was foreign to Remi. Normally, she was more at home outside than inside. She especially loved mountains—or at least, the mountains back home in Colorado. These lush, evergreen-choked Smokies were as different from her dramatic soaring Rockies as a black bear was from a polar bear. Both were beautiful and special in completely different ways. But this unfamiliar wilderness seemed to be closing in on her, thickening the air with a sense of menace and filling her with dread.

Was this how Allison Downs had felt when she'd hiked through the Shenandoah National Park and was never seen again?

Or Melanie Shepherd in the Dry Tortugas?

Or even her own sister, when their high school senior class trip had gone so horribly wrong?

"Stop being a spoilsport, Remi. That waterfall is supposed to be gorgeous by moonlight and I'm tired of being stuck here in this stupid tent. No one else's parents make them go to bed at ten o'clock. It's embarrassing." Becca tried to push through the tent flap, but Remi blocked her way.

"It's too dangerous," Remi told her. "Daddy said it's the wrong time of year to go up that trail. The water level is too high and the rocks are slippery with ice. Besides, since when do you care about nature, other than those stupid constellations you love to look at?" She studied her sister. "You're meeting someone, aren't you? Some boy."

Becca rolled her eyes. "You're just jealous because no one asked you to party."

"I knew it. Who? Billy Hendricks?"

Another eye roll. "Oh, please. Billy's like a lapdog, panting at my heels. What's the challenge in that? I've hooked a much bigger fish than silly Billy." She laughed and tried to move past Remi. But Remi grabbed the sleeve of her sister's jacket and held on.

"Becca, stop. You're going to ruin this whole trip. If Daddy finds out that you're sneaking out, especially to meet a guy, he'll take us back home early."

Her sister's mouth tightened. "If anyone is ruining this stupid trip, it's Dad, not me. At least the other chaperones have the sense to leave their kids alone. No one else's parents are in a tent right next to theirs. He's smothering us."

"He loves us. He wants to keep us safe."

"From what? Last time I looked, cancer wasn't lurking in the woods."

Remi drew in a sharp breath. "That's low, Becca. And completely unfair."

Remorse flashed in Becca's light brown eyes, which were a mirror of her own. For a moment, Remi thought her sister was going to give in, maybe even apologize for using their mother's recent death from breast cancer as a barb in an argument. But Becca suddenly shoved her backward, forcing her to let go of the jacket.

Becca's hands tightened into fists at her sides, a clear warning for Remi not to try to stop her again. "There are fifty kids out here in this stupid camp-

*ground and ten chaperones. Ten! We can't even skin
a knee without stumbling over some anxious parent
with a first aid kit. You'd think we were still in elementary school instead of planning which colleges
to go to in the fall."*

"Becca—"

*"This is your fault. Our entire trip has been a di-
saster, all because you told Dad the school needed
another chaperone. You know how overprotective he
is. You should have kept your mouth shut. And you're
going to keep it shut this time or I'll make you regret
it. You owe me this. Leave me alone. Let me have
some fun."* She flung open the tent flap and disappeared into the night.

Remi swallowed hard at the memory of her sister's
long, wavy dark hair rippling out behind her. That
was the last time she'd ever seen her.

A little farther down the trail, the trees and brush
on her right thinned out and then disappeared alto-
gether. A fifty-foot break revealed endless miles of
dense, forest-covered peaks and the occasional bald
where disease or insects had killed large swaths of
trees and undergrowth. Charred earth and blackened
trunks spoke of wildfires that had ravaged this area in
recent years. And through it all, little white puffs of
mist rose toward the sky like ancient smoke signals,
adding to the blue-white haze that gave this section
of the Appalachians their name.

She stopped, mesmerized. Not by the scenery.
But by thoughts of her sister so long ago. A lifetime
ago. Had Becca made it to this section of the AT the

night she disappeared? Was this the spot her killer had chosen for his attack? Had she looked out over this beautiful vista underneath a bright full moon, completely unaware of the danger that crept up on her from behind?

If Remi was the killer, this was where she'd make her move. It was remote, isolated and empty. She hadn't passed anyone since leaving the trail shelter this morning, miles from here. It was too cold to attract many hikers at this time of year. The crowds of northbound thru-hikers, or NOBOs, with dreams of completing the two-thousand-mile trek in one year from Georgia to Maine wouldn't clog the trail until spring. The lack of NOBOs to contend with was one of the reasons the ill-fated senior class trip had been planned for midwinter instead of closer to graduation.

Remi could easily imagine Becca standing here, memorizing the way moonlight spilled its light across the peaks and valleys, so she could tell her tree-hugging twin all about it when she returned to the tent. Or looking up at the stars, so much easier to see on the mountain, away from what Becca called the "light pollution" in the city. More likely, she could have been standing here waiting for whatever boy she'd gone off to meet. The identity of her secret admirer had never been discovered. It could have been Billy Hendricks, even though she'd denied it. Or the golden boy of their senior class, Garrett Weber, except that he already had a girlfriend at the time. Whoever it was, none of the boys at camp would admit to meeting her in the woods. Why would they? They would have made themselves suspects in her disappearance.

Remi studied the gap, a chill skittering up her spine. This was definitely a perfect place for a trap, an ambush. The steep drop would have blocked her sister's escape to the west. Thick trees and brush to the east would make it difficult to get very far before being caught. If someone was behind her, she'd have to shove past them to run up or down the trail.

What happened to you, Becca?

Scuffling noises sounded behind her.

She whirled around, yanking her gun out of her pocket and bringing it up in one swift motion.

Chapter Two

A hulking, dark-haired man dressed in green camou-flage stared at her from twenty feet away, his face a mask of menace and hatred. He suddenly shoved his hand into his pocket.

"Freeze!" she yelled.

Ignoring her order, he tugged at something dark and metallic in his pocket that seemed to be caught in the fabric. *A gun!*

"No!" another man's voice yelled from off to her left somewhere.

Camo-guy yanked the gun free.

Remi squeezed the trigger. *Bam! Bam!*

Camo-guy's eyes widened in disbelief and he dropped like a rock. Remi jerked toward her left to face the next threat. A second man barreled into her, slamming them both to the ground, crushing her right shoulder. Agony knifed through her. She gritted her teeth and tried to push him away.

He rolled off her.

Fighting through the blinding pain, she flopped onto her back and tried to force her right arm to cooperate so she could point her gun at him. Except he wasn't there. And she didn't have her gun.

The sound of someone running had her turning her head to see her attacker drop to his knees beside the man she'd shot. He moaned and writhed on the ground, clutching his side.

She frantically looked around for her pistol. There, a few feet away. Her SIG was under a bush, where it must have landed when she was knocked down. Clutching her hurt arm against her chest, she scrambled forward on her knees. Awkwardly leaning in, she thrust her left hand beneath the branches, fingers scrabbling against the dirt.

"Oh, no, you don't," a deep voice snarled behind her. Her attacker was back.

She dived for the gun.

He grabbed her right ankle and yanked backward.

She cried out in frustration and kicked her legs. One of them slammed against his thigh. It was like hitting a solid rock. The impact had her clenching her teeth.

He swore. Maybe she'd managed to hurt him, too.

She kicked again, this time knocking his hand off her ankle.

She lunged forward, desperately reaching for her SIG Sauer.

Strong fingers clamped around both her calves like vice grips. He jerked her backward, so hard and fast that her jacket and shirt bunched up beneath her. Dirt and rocks scraped her belly, tracing a fiery burn across her skin.

Twisting around, she brought up her knee toward his groin as she swung a left hook at him.

He dived sideways, avoiding her knee, but not her fist. The blow caught him hard on his temple, making him grunt. But it didn't slow him down. He threw himself on top of her, pinning her to the ground.

She bucked her hips, trying to throw him off while she struggled to coil her left hand into a fist for round two. Good grief, he was strong, a powerhouse of muscles that made her Pilates workouts seem like a pathetic waste of time. She could probably outrun him. Running was one of the few things where she excelled. But she had to get him off her first. She drew back her fist again.

He flipped her onto her stomach.

Hot lava boiled across the nerve endings in her battered shoulder. Bile rose in her throat. She could feel him fumbling for something, his hips moving alarmingly against her bottom as he turned to the side. Was he going to rape her?

"Let me go." She struggled harder, pushing through the pain.

He reared up and jerked her arms back. Agony seared her shoulder. She cried out. Dark spots swam in her vision.

The feel of cold steel against her wrists had her stiffening. He was trying to handcuff her! She twisted and snaked against the ground, desperately trying to keep him from getting the cuffs into position. Her shoulder felt as if it was being shredded with a hot poker, but she couldn't let up. If he got those cuffs fastened, she was as good as dead. Her vision clouded. She was close to passing out from the pain.

"Fight, Remi. You can do this!" Her sister's voice echoed in her mind.

The ratcheting sound of the cuffs locking into place sounded behind her. He shoved his hands into her jacket pockets, took her cell phone. Then he ran his hands quickly up and down her body. She cursed at him and tried to arch away.

"Stay there. Don't move." The command from her captor sounded more like an angry growl than an order. His weight lifted off her and once again he was gone.

She collapsed against the ground, the fight draining out of her. There was nothing else she could do. She squeezed her eyes shut. *I'm so sorry, Daddy. Please forgive me, Becca.* A whimper clogged her throat. *Becca.* Her sometimes sweet, always impetuous, infuriating twin. Maybe it was fitting that they'd both die in the same place, together as always, cradle to grave.

Remi lay unmoving. What was her assailant doing now? Without him weighing her down and her struggling against him, the agony in her shoulder became bearable. The black fog dissipated and the fuzziness in her head evaporated.

A low murmur had her turning her head. The man who'd cuffed her was on his knees again beside his partner in crime, saying something to him. His neon orange backpack strained across his broad shoulders, the color contrasting sharply with his black pants and black shirt. The wounded man writhed on the ground, his teeth bared like a rabid animal caught in a trap.

"Idiot! Stop wasting time. Get up while he's distracted. Run!"

Her sister's voice was so loud inside Remi's head that she half expected to see her forever-seventeen features twisted with fury.

I'm so sorry, Becca. It's all my fault. Everything is my fault.

Pent-up grief swept through her like a tsunami, obliterating everything in its path. It drowned her in a sea of sorrow that was just as fresh now as when she was a teenager. Losing both her mother and her sister the same year had nearly destroyed her. The death of her father a little over a year later *had* destroyed her, or at least, the person she used to be. She'd had to remake herself into someone new just to survive. A harder, tougher Remi Jordan. Or so she'd thought. Yet here she lay, helpless, about to die. *You're right, Becca. I'm an idiot.*

"Stop feeling sorry for yourself, Remi. Get your lazy butt up and run! Now! You owe me!"

You owe me. Her sister was right. She had to at least try. Remi tried to jerk upright, then gasped at the white-hot pain that shot through her shoulder. She shuddered and braced her forehead against the cold ground, gulping in short breaths of arctic air.

"Get up!" Becca yelled again.

Remi drew a ragged breath and awkwardly wiggled her body. Without the use of her hands to push herself up, it took a ridiculous amount of time to make it to a sitting position. But at least with her hands cuffed behind her back, the pressure on her shoulder was making it go blessedly numb. Maybe she could do this, after all.

She braced herself to try to stand, and risked a quick glance at the two men. The one who'd cuffed her had his backpack on the ground beside him and had taken out a first aid kit. With one hand pressing gauze bandages against the injured man's side, he sat back and reached his other hand toward his waist.

Remi stiffened, expecting him to pull out a gun, maybe even hers. Instead, he lifted the edge of his jacket to reveal a thick black belt.

A *utility* belt.

With various leather holders clipped to it, like the kind that held handcuffs.

And a two-way radio.

A horrible suspicion swept through her, freezing her in place.

He grabbed the radio and pressed one of the buttons on the side. As if he sensed her watching him, his gaze flew to hers. The radio crackled and he spoke into the transmitter.

"This is Special Agent Duncan McKenzie. I located the woman the witness at the shelter reported seeing with a gun. But not before she shot a hiker. I need a medical crew up here, ASAP."

The blood drained from Remi's face, leaving her cold and shaking. Her gaze flew to the man she'd shot. He was pale and still on the forest floor, his eyes closed. And beside him, hanging out of his pocket, was the gun he'd pulled on her.

Except it wasn't a gun.

It was a cell phone.

Dear God. What had she done?

Chapter Three

Hunching in his jacket against the bitter wind, Duncan paused behind the unfamiliar SUV in the gravel lot by the office trailer. The vehicle's plain exterior and dark color would typically help it blend in and avoid being noticed. Not here. Surrounded by white vehicles with green stripes down their sides and the brown National Park Service arrowhead shield on their doors, the SUV stuck out like a white-tailed deer in a herd of elk.

The license plate was federal government issue, but not the kind used by the NPS. All Duncan knew for sure was that whatever alphabet agency was here, they hadn't simply dropped by on their way someplace else. Nestled deep inside the Great Smoky Mountains National Park, this satellite office was miles from the nearest town, Gatlinburg. The steep, winding access road was a challenge during the summer, nearly impossible during the winter without a four-wheel drive. Which meant their visitor was here on purpose. Something big must be going on, and Duncan aimed to find out what that was.

He jogged up the salted concrete steps at the end of the long trailer to the only door, a solid steel monstrosity designed to keep out the occasional curious black bear. The deep scratches in the prison-gray paint proved just how solid, and necessary, that precaution was. Even the huge metal storage shed at the end of the lot was reinforced with heavy steel bars. Working in the wilderness was dangerous in more ways than one. He pulled open the door and stepped inside.

Seventies-era dark wood paneling sucked up most of the light, in spite of wide windows set high up on the longest opposing walls. Four desks were tucked end to end beneath those windows, leaving a center aisle of worn rust-colored shag carpet. His boss, Yeong Lee, faced him from behind another, larger desk at the end of the aisle. Across from him, occupying the two metal folding chairs reserved for visitors, were a large black man in a charcoal-gray suit and a petite Caucasian woman with long blond hair cascading down her back.

As Duncan hung his jacket and gloves on hooks beside the door, he exchanged greetings with the only other people inside, Rangers Nick Grady and Oliver McAlister. Skinny freckle-faced Grady was a green-around-the-gills new recruit, while white-haired McAlister, with his gravelly smoker's voice and stout frame, was a permanent fixture in the park. Dubbed Pup and Pops, the two were sitting together to the right of the door at McAlister's desk. As usual,

Pops was mentoring Grady about something on the computer screen.

Duncan paused beside McAlister. "Thanks for helping me out this morning. Did the prisoner give you any trouble?"

He shook his head. "No trouble at all and no thanks needed. If you hadn't been here at 0-dark-thirty and taken the call for us, we'd have been the ones assigned to head up there, anyway. What's the story on the hiker? Did he make it?"

"He got lucky. The bullet passed through the fleshy part of his side. Lost a lot of blood and they've got him on IV antibiotics to stave off infection. But he's expected to make a full recovery." He motioned toward the couple across from Lee. "Which agency decided to pay us a visit? Any idea why they're here?"

McAlister exchanged a surprised look with Grady, his bushy eyebrows climbing like albino caterpillars to his hairline. "You don't recognize the woman from this morning?"

Duncan frowned and studied her as best he could from across the room. The long blond hair did remind him of the shooter's hair. But since McAlister had taken her into custody, that wasn't possible. Was it? She lifted her left hand, motioning in the air as she spoke to Lee. She also gave Duncan his first clear view of a royal blue shirtsleeve and the cream-colored jacket folded over the arm of her chair. He sucked in a sharp breath, his hands fisting at his sides. It was her. The combination of blond hair, blue shirt and off-white jacket couldn't be a coincidence.

If he'd been a second slower this morning, he'd either be sporting some seriously bruised ribs thanks to his Kevlar vest, or he'd have had his head blown off, depending on the aim of the woman sitting in that chair.

"Why isn't she locked up?" Without waiting for McAlister's reply, he strode up the aisle to Lee's desk and turned to face the woman once again. Except, this time, she wasn't pointing a gun at him.

The white sling cradling her right arm forestalled the angry words he'd been about to say. Instead, suspicion heavy in his tone, he demanded, "What happened to you?" She wouldn't be the first suspect to fake an injury to delay being booked into jail.

Her dark brows rose. "You did."

"Is that supposed to be funny? Because I find it incredibly offensive."

She held her left hand in front of her in a placating gesture. "I'm just stating facts. When you slammed me to the ground, you dislocated my shoulder." She shrugged, then winced and clasped her left hand over her right shoulder as if she was in pain.

He wasn't buying her act. And he sure as certain wasn't letting her version of events go unchallenged. "I think what you meant to say was that I tackled you to keep from being shot, after you'd just shot an unarmed man and then turned your pistol on me."

A red flush crept up her neck. "I thought the hiker had a gun. And you attacked me. I was protecting myself."

"The only one attacking anyone up there was you."

He tapped the lump on his temple where she'd punched him, which he knew already had a visible bruise.

Her jaw tightened, but she didn't respond.

He waved toward the back right corner of the trailer. "Why isn't she locked up in the holding cell? Or on her way to jail courtesy of Gatlinburg PD? She could have killed Kurt Vale."

"Could have?" Her eyes widened. "Then...he's alive?"

The hopeful tone of her voice sounded false to him. "The time for concern would have been *before* you pulled the trigger and shot an innocent man. But if you're asking whether you managed to kill him, the answer is no. I just left him at the hospital after the doctor stitched him up."

"I'm glad he's okay."

Ignoring her, he turned to his boss. "What's going on here?"

Lee addressed the man silently observing them from the other side of the desk. "FBI Supervisory Special Agent Leon Johnson, meet Special Agent Duncan McKenzie, criminal investigator with the National Park Service."

Johnson held his hand out without bothering to pry his generous frame out of the ridiculously small folding chair beneath him.

Duncan leaned across the desk and shook the agent's hand, but his attention once again turned to the woman. Four hours ago she'd shot a hiker. Now she was parked beside an FBI agent. Why? Since he regularly studied the FBI's ten most-wanted-fugitives list, he knew she wasn't on it. But she must have done something pretty dang bad to warrant the FBI showing up, especially this soon after the shooting. So why wasn't she handcuffed? Or in the cell while the agent spoke to his boss?

"I'm a little lost." Duncan glanced back and forth between Lee and Johnson. "Since our shooting suspect is sitting beside an FBI agent, I assume there's something else going on that involves her, besides what happened this morning. Can someone catch me up here?"

"What's going on," Johnson said, "is that your shooting suspect is one of our agents. She was off duty, supposed to be on vacation, not running around shooting people."

Duncan stared at him in shock. The woman from this morning's shooting was a Fed? A fellow law-enforcement officer? He hadn't gotten to speak to her after the shooting. He didn't even know her name. He'd been too busy trying to keep Kurt Vale from bleeding out. As soon as McAlister and Grady had arrived to take her into custody, he hadn't given her another thought. Instead, he'd helped the medics get Vale down the mountain to the waiting ambulance.

"You're FBI?" He couldn't quite wrap his head around that.

She stood and held out her left hand, since her right one was in the sling. "Special Agent Remi Jordan."

He eyed her hand like he would a poisonous snake.

She took the hint and sat back down.

Johnson laboriously rose to his feet and tugged

his suit jacket into place. "Special Agent Jordan has waived her right to an attorney and has declined my offer to stay here with her. She has assured me that she's prepared to fully cooperate with your investigation. Isn't that right?"

She gave him a curt nod, but didn't meet his gaze.

"I've already taken her badge," Johnson said. "And your crime scene unit logged her gun as evidence. She's now on administrative leave, pending the results of your investigation. If either of you gentlemen need anything further from my office, let me know." He tapped a white business card sitting on the desk. "Now, if you'll excuse me, I need to get back to Knoxville." He grabbed his coat from a peg behind Lee's desk and then shrugged into it as he headed toward the door.

Duncan watched the man leave, distaste burning like acid in his throat. For the first time since the shooting earlier today, he felt a tug of sympathy for the woman sitting on the other side of the desk. No matter what she'd told Johnson, the man was her boss. It was his duty to look out for her. He should have insisted that she get a lawyer, or brought one with him. Lee sure would have. He'd fight like a rabid bobcat to defend every member of his team. Justice would be served, of course. But he'd do everything he could to ensure that his officers' rights were protected.

Lee pushed back his chair and stood. "Special Agent Jordan, with you getting that shoulder patched up and your boss asking us to wait until he got here to talk, we haven't had much of a chance to discuss the details of the shooting. Special Agent McKenzie will take your statement. In the meantime, my stomach is eating a hole through my spine. I'll head down the mountain and get us all some lunch. Any dietary restrictions or preferences I should know about?"

Her expression turned wary as she obviously debated whether or not to trust him. From the way her own boss had just acted, Duncan couldn't blame her.

"That's very nice of you," she told Lee. "Thank you. And no, no restrictions. Whatever you get is fine and much appreciated."

"All right. I'll be back in an hour, give or take." He grabbed his gloves and heavy jacket hanging on the wall behind his chair and motioned toward Pup and Pops. "Grady, you're my pack mule this trip," he called out. "You can chauffer me into town while I check my email on my phone."

From the grin on the kid's eager face, he must have thought he'd won the lottery. He jumped up so fast that he almost overturned his chair.

Pops shook his head, but a smile played around his lips as he turned to his computer monitor. Grady started peppering Lee with questions about procedures and reports before Lee could even close the door behind them. The pained expression on his face when he glanced back had Duncan wondering if his boss already regretted his decision to take his newest employee with him into town.

Duncan motioned toward the back wall. His anger had given way to grudging curiosity now that he knew his suspect was in law enforcement. With a federal agent involved, he could understand why Lee had chosen not to turn her over to the local police. Instead, the NPS would handle it as an interagency courtesy—at least for now. It was up to Duncan to get the answers to the questions that had been rolling around in his head from the moment he'd taken a hiker's call early this morning.

"Special Agent Jordan, if you'll take a seat in the other room, I need to grab my laptop to take notes."

She stood and waved toward the reinforced-glass and steel door on the far right. "In there?"

He followed her gesture. "Ah, no. That's the holding cell. In spite of what I may have said earlier about locking you up, in the eight years that I've worked here, we've never once used that room for its intended purpose. It's stuffed with boxes of office supplies and old case files." He motioned toward the door on the far left. "I meant the conference room. I'm sure you were shown where the restroom was earlier." He motioned toward the middle door. "If you need—"

"No, thank you." She moved stiffly past him and marched into the conference room like a prisoner heading to death row.

Chapter Four

When Special Agent Remi Jordan passed Duncan, he was struck by how petite she was. The top of her head barely reached his chin. In blue jeans and a simple blue blouse, without a jacket to provide bulk, she probably didn't tip a hundred pounds on a scale. Her right arm being trussed up in a sling only emphasized her vulnerability. Seeing her this way, with this morning's drama stripped away, and no gun, Duncan realized she appeared utterly defenseless. And he had the inexplicable urge to offer his protection, to reassure her that everything was going to be all right.

That would be foolish and wrong on so many levels, especially because it would probably be a lie.

As a trained officer, she should have used deadly force as a last resort. Instead, she'd used it as her first response. She'd shot an unarmed man while off duty, on vacation, according to her boss, with no provocation that Duncan had seen. She could be looking at charges of attempted murder, attempted manslaughter or, the very least, assault. If by some miracle she avoided charges and didn't go to prison, she'd likely still lose her job with the FBI. And she'd almost certainly face financial ruin in the civil courts. With another law-enforcement officer as a witness, Vale could ride that gravy train all the way to the bank.

Duncan stood in the doorway, watching her consider the four padded wooden chairs, the square vinyl-topped table that was more appropriate for playing cards than for a conference or an interview. But like everything else in this trailer, the table and chairs met the main requirement—they were small enough to fit the tiny space.

She apparently decided not to bother with a chair. Instead, she moved to the lone window at the other end of the room. Facing away from him, she stared through the glass at the snow, which was falling again.

"Special Agent Jordan?"

She glanced over her shoulder. "Remi, please. Calling me Special Agent every time you ask me a question is going to get really old, really fast, for both of us."

"Remi. Unusual name. Is that short for something?"

"Remilyn, after my grandmother. But my mom's the only person who ever called me that."

"Called? Then she's—"

"She passed away when I was seventeen. Breast cancer."

The slight wobble in her voice told him that she'd loved her mother, and that her death—he was guessing eight or nine years ago—still hurt.

He counted his blessings that both his parents were still alive and doing well. He couldn't imagine not being able to drop by their cabin, share a beer with his father or ask his mother's advice.

"My condolences," he said, and meant it.

She gave him a crisp nod. "Thank you."

He waved toward the sling. "While I wouldn't have changed the actions I took this morning, I do regret that you got hurt. What did the doctor say about your shoulder?"

She hesitated, the wary expression she'd given Lee firmly back in place. "The EMT rotated it into the socket. It's fine."

He waited, but when she didn't elaborate, he asked, "You were taken to the hospital, right? You were seen by a doctor?"

"All a doctor would have done was tell me to schedule an appointment with a physical therapist. I had the EMT treat me in the back of the ambulance, and told him I didn't want to go to the hospital."

She didn't *want* to go? She shouldn't have been given a choice. She was under arrest, her well-being the responsibility of the National Park Service while in their custody. McAlister and Grady should have *made* her go to the hospital, with them as her armed escorts.

"What did the EMT give you for pain?" He didn't want her to suffer. But equally important, he didn't want a defense attorney down the road having her statement tossed out on the basis that she was heavily medicated, which affected her mental state and her ability to understand her rights.

"I haven't had a chance to take anything," she said. "My purse is locked in the trunk of my car at the trailhead. I don't have any pills with me here."

"I've got some ibuprofen in my desk if you want."

She frowned as if puzzled by his offer. Had she expected him to chain her to a chair and allow her only bread and water?

"I'd appreciate that. The shoulder does ache a bit."

"If you prefer to go to the hospital for an MRI—which I strongly recommend—and to get a prescription for the pain—"

"Over-the-counter pills will be fine."

Visions of future defense attorneys were still dancing in his head. She really should go to the hospital. But it was her shoulder, after all. Not a head injury. And she'd been given medical treatment by the EMT. It was probably safe to take her statement.

"I'll be right back."

"Special Agent McKenzie?"

"If I'm calling you Remi then you have to call me Duncan." He added a smile that he was far from feeling. But keeping things friendly would make the interview go much more smoothly. Orders from her boss to cooperate would go only so far if she had something to hide about why she was in the mountains with a gun. He'd start out playing good cop and see how things went.

She gestured toward the side of his head. "Duncan.

I really am sorry about everything that happened. I hope that doesn't hurt too much."

It took him a second to realize she was talking about punching him. His grin was genuine this time. "You've got a wicked left hook."

Her answering smile seemed reluctant, but also genuine. "I'm right-handed. You got lucky."

He laughed. "So I did. No worries. We'll talk everything out and then decide where to go from there. Okay?"

She blew out a shuddering breath, her face relaxing with relief. "Sounds good."

When he reached his desk, he pulled his laptop from the bottom drawer just as his cell phone buzzed. He took it out of his pocket and checked the screen. It was Lee. A quick glance toward the open door of the conference room confirmed that Remi was still standing at the window, looking out. Duncan plopped his laptop on the desk and sat down to take the call.

"Hey, boss. Did you shove Grady into a snowbank yet to shut him up?" he teased.

"Have you started interviewing Special Agent Jordan yet?"

The terseness of Lee's tone immediately had Duncan on alert. "About to. Why?"

"Johnson had his assistant send me an email. I forwarded it to you. It makes for some interesting reading. Skim it before you talk to her."

"Why?"

"Humor me." The line clicked.

Duncan sighed and flipped open the laptop. There

were fifteen unread emails since just this morning. Most had to do with the case he was in the process of closing, a string of vehicle break-ins and vandalism he'd been working for the past four months. The small band of local teens behind the crimes was in jail. Now it was just a matter of paperwork and testimony once the trials were underway—assuming they even went to trial.

None of the kids had criminal records. And knowing his friend Clay Perry, the district attorney, Duncan figured he'd likely plead them out. Clay was a father of five and had a seemingly endless supply of patience and empathy for kids—whether they deserved it or not.

Their parents would pay hefty fines and the little hoodlums would soon be back on the streets. And Duncan would have to arrest them all over again a few months down the road when they started up again, or turned to other types of crimes. It was an endless cycle, one that he and Clay often debated over cold beers, sizzling steaks and friendly poker games.

Not seeing anything particularly urgent in the subject lines of the emails, he clicked on the one from his boss. The message was brief, simply telling Duncan to read the attachment.

It took half a minute for the memory-hogging document to load on his screen. When it did, he frowned. Why would Remi's boss feel it was necessary to send this? And why would Lee want Duncan to read it prior to the interview? How could this possibly be relevant to the shooting?

He let out a long breath and dutifully clicked through several pages, quickly scanning the headings of each section. He began to wonder whether he'd missed the punch line to an inside joke. Then, five pages in, he quit scanning. He leaned closer to the monitor and read every single word. Then he went back to the beginning and read it all again.

Chapter Five

Remi's fingers tightened against the windowsill as she watched the snow falling even harder outside the conference room window. She was trying to find her center, calm her nerves in anticipation of the upcoming inquisition. But so far it wasn't working. She'd interviewed suspects dozens of times over the years. But she'd never once been on the other side of the table. And she wasn't looking forward to the experience. Especially since she couldn't even explain to herself what had happened this morning.

She was sick at the thought that she could have shot an unarmed man. But every time she replayed the confrontation in her mind, the memories ticked through like the frames of a movie, replaying exactly the same way that she remembered, never changing.

Scuffling sounded behind her.

She turned, gun in hand, finger on the frame, not the trigger.

A man in camouflage, a look of such menace on his face that she had zero doubt he was the one who'd been stalking her. Or was he just angry that she was pointing a gun at him?

She told him to freeze.

He pulled a gun out of his pocket. It had gotten caught on the fabric of his jacket. But he still pulled it out. She could picture it, clearly. He couldn't have been more than twenty feet away. It was a Glock 19, 9 mm, a weapon she'd seen many times during her career.

She'd moved her finger to the trigger, because she had to. Shoot or be shot. Kill or be killed. She'd fired, in self-defense, only one shot, because there was another threat, off to her left.

Duncan. Knowing he was there had likely distracted her just enough to save Vale's life. Normally, she was an excellent marksman.

He'd tackled her, knocking her pistol loose.

A few minutes later, the man she'd shot lay on the ground, a cell phone hanging out of his pocket. The phone was black. So was the gun. But the first was a rectangle, the last a pistol. Nothing alike. She could never mistake the two.

Could she?

Her knuckles grew white against the wooden sill. Could she have been so distracted by thoughts of her sister, by the same grief and anger that had plagued her for years, that she'd seen something that wasn't there? Had she wanted so badly to believe that the man in front of her was the one responsible for the disappearances, that her mind had played tricks on her?

Five years. She'd been in law enforcement for five years. She was far from being an expert, still new in many ways. But she found it hard to believe that after all that time she could screw up this badly. The man, this Kurt Vale guy, had to have had a gun. But if he did, then where was the gun now?

"Hello? Remi? Anybody home?"

She blinked, bringing the room, and Duncan, into focus. She instinctively scrambled back several steps to put more distance between her and this rather tall, intimidating man in front of her.

His eyes widened and he, too, stepped back, giving her more space. "I didn't mean to startle you." His jaw tightened and his dark blue eyes looked down toward her side.

She followed his gaze and realized her left hand was balled into a fist and half-raised, as if she was going to slug him again. Her face flushed hot and she forced her fingers to uncurl. "Sorry. You...surprised me."

"Like Kurt Vale surprised you up on the ridge? Right before you shot him?"

Her face grew hotter. "He had a gun."

"The only gun I saw was in your hand."

"That's because you saw my gun first and assumed that I was the threat. You probably never looked at him after that. If you hadn't attacked me, you'd have noticed that he was pulling out a weapon, too. A Glock 19, 9 mm."

He spread his hands in a conciliatory gesture. "I'd like to believe you. I really would. But it's hard to support your story when only one gun was found—yours. A crime scene unit processed the scene. The evidence they collected where Vale was lying included bloody gauze and a broken cell phone. That's it."

"Broken?"

"From the fall. The phone fell out of his pocket. Hit some rocks on the ground beside him, which shattered the screen."

"Why did it fall out, unless he was pulling something else out of his pocket and knocked it loose?"

His brows arched. "Like his hands? To hold them up and show you he was unarmed?"

She pressed her lips together.

He sighed. "Let's take it step by step." He motioned toward the table, which had a laptop sitting on it. Across from that were a bottle of water and a container of over-the-counter pain pills. Both were open, their caps lying on the table. "I imagine that shoulder's hurting quite a bit. Why don't you get some pain meds on board, before we officially start?"

"He had a gun," she insisted.

"I'm sure you thought that he did."

There was no judgment in his tone, no condemnation. Instead, he sounded surprisingly empathetic. Which of course meant that he was good at his job, good at defusing her anger, making her feel less defensive. Not because he cared about her or felt solidarity with a fellow law-enforcement officer, but because he wanted her in an agreeable mood so she'd answer his questions. She wanted to be angry at him for using interview tricks and techniques on her. Instead, she couldn't help but admire him for it. If she was in his position, she'd do the exact same thing.

She stepped around him and sat in the chair with its back to the door. She figured she'd hear the door if someone opened it. And more important, she didn't want to turn her back on Duncan, who was still standing by the window where she'd left him, watching her as if he was trying to figure her out. Fine. She'd just watch him right back.

Taking her time with the pills, she studied him from beneath her lashes. He was a handsome man, no denying that. He wasn't much older than her, maybe thirty or so. His tanned face was a study in angles and hard edges a camera would love, made even more interesting by the combination of nearly jet-black hair and midnight-blue eyes. But it was his height—about six foot three—and those broad shoulders and toned, muscular body that made her hyperaware of her own small stature. If he was just a man, and she was just a woman, she'd have probably been excited and intrigued by his size and strength. But as a federal agent with her freedom and her career on the line, he intimidated her, which made her resentful.

Two long strides later, he was sitting across from her, pulling his laptop toward him. His gaze settled on her with an intensity that was unnerving. "Are you sure you don't want me to take you to the hospital?"

"I'm fine," she assured him. But from the skeptical look on his face, she didn't think he believed her.

"Everything in here is recorded." He waved toward the camera anchored near the ceiling on the wall to her left. "For your protection and mine."

"I saw the camera as soon as I walked in. I assume

someone is also watching us through the one-way glass in the top of the door behind me."

"They could if they wanted. But I think Pops is more interested in finishing his reports so he can leave on time today."

"Pops?"

"The only ranger in the office right now, the older guy, Oliver McAlister. We call him Pops because he's been here longer than anyone else and treats us all like his kids."

He smiled again, making her wonder if he was trying to put her at ease or whether he was one of those people who always seemed happy. Those kind of people got on her nerves and made her fingers itch for her gun. Not having its familiar weight on her hip made her feel naked and vulnerable, a feeling she didn't like one bit.

"Please state your name and address for the video."

"Remilyn Jordan." She listed her street address. "Greenwood Village, Colorado."

"Colorado? I thought you lived in Tennessee and worked out of the Knoxville field office."

She shook her head. "I work in Denver. Johnson came over from the nearest field office, the one in Knoxville. But he's not my regular boss. He's my pseudoboss while I'm here under investigation."

"Got it. Greenwood Village, Colorado. Can't say I've ever heard of it."

"Outside of Denver, about an hour from Boulder, give or take."

"I bet it's beautiful there. Great mountain views of the Rockies."

"It's beautiful," she conceded.

"But you decided to come here on vacation, to another mountain range."

"Is that a question?"

He smiled again. "Before we go any further, I need to remind you about your rights."

"We can skip that part. *Pops* Mirandized me on the way down the mountain."

"I figured he had. But I still have to tell you your rights on camera. Like I said, for your protection and mine."

Not seeing the point in arguing, she suffered through his recitation of the Miranda warning.

"Do you understand each of these rights as I've explained them to you?" he asked.

She nodded.

"You have to say it," he reminded her.

"Yes." She sighed. "Yes, I understand my rights. Yes, I'm willing to speak to you without a lawyer. Can we just talk this out and get it over with?"

The plastic water bottle crackled between her hands. She hadn't even realized that she'd picked it up. She set it down.

"I can't imagine you driving all the way here from Colorado. Did you fly in? Then rent a car while you're in town?"

"Actually, no. I drove. As you're well aware, I brought a weapon with me. Driving was easier than going through the headaches that declaring my weapon would require on a plane."

"Especially since you're here off duty, on vacation."

"Exactly."

He opened his laptop, typed for a moment. "Where are you staying?"

"A motel a few streets back from the main drag in Gatlinburg." She told him the name.

"You've been in town how long?"

"A couple of days."

"And what have you been doing every day while you've been here?"

She hesitated. How much should she reveal? Cooperating was her best chance at trying to avoid any charges. But would her purpose in being here help her, or hurt her?

"Do you need me to repeat the question?" he asked.

"I've been hiking trails in the Great Smoky Mountains National Park, mainly the Appalachian Trail."

"Every day?"

"Every day."

"Why?"

She blinked. "The same reason anyone hikes, I suppose. To see nature, the beautiful scenery. To get away from the pressures of my job. The Smokies aren't at all like the mountains back home. I wanted to see something different."

"It's February. The temperatures are hovering in the twenties at night, forties and fifties during the day. And that's in town. Up here at these elevations, it gets even colder. Not to mention the ice and snow. Want to try again? Why are you hiking in freezing temps in the middle of winter?"

"I'm not the only hiker up here at this time of year. I've seen several."

"There are some, yes. Not many. What I'm interested in is why *you're* here at one of the worst times of year to be outside in the park."

She stared at him, her left hand beneath the table now, her fingers curling against her palm. "I like solitude. I like to be alone. And I don't mind the cold."

His silence told her he wasn't buying her answer. He waited, probably hoping she'd feel compelled to fill the silence, divulge something she didn't want to share. But she knew interview techniques. She wasn't saying anything unless she was answering a specific question.

"Why did you shoot Kurt Vale?"

She sucked in a breath, thrown off-kilter by the abrupt change in the conversation. But rather than rush to defend herself, which could have led to her spilling all sorts of things, she took a moment to regain her composure. When she was sure she was in control, she said, "I was standing at a gap in the trees, admiring the scenery. I'd heard someone following me earlier, so when I heard a noise behind me, I naturally whirled around and drew my gun. To defend myself."

"What did Vale do?"

"He drew his gun, a Glock."

"He didn't have a gun. I saw him standing twenty

feet away from you. And I saw you, holding your SIG Sauer, pointing it at an unarmed man."

"That's not what happened. You saw him, then me. And as soon as you realized I had my gun out, you no longer looked at him. At that point, you deemed that I was the threat, and you charged at me. You didn't look back at Vale and see that he'd pulled out a gun and was about to shoot me. I yelled at him to freeze. He didn't. I had no choice but to fire my weapon."

He leaned forward, crossing his forearms on top of the table. "Here's the thing, Remi. The only way that story holds water is if we found a gun at the scene, this Glock you say he had. But the only gun we found was your SIG Sauer, the one that I saw you aim at Kurt Vale, the one I saw you fire."

She shook her head. "You're wrong. If your crime scene techs didn't find Vale's gun, they missed it. They should go back and look harder. It has to be there."

"After I knocked you to the ground to keep you from shooting an unarmed man a second time, I rendered first aid to the victim. He was shot in the side and was losing a lot of blood. He was in no condition to run off somewhere and hide his alleged gun, then run back and lie down, all in the span of the few seconds it took me to knock you down and then go to him. The only items he had with him were his wallet, his car keys and his cell phone. I contend that the cell phone is what you saw in his hand, not a pistol."

"You're wrong."

He held his hands up. "I want to believe you. I want to be wrong. Convince me."

She tapped her fingers against her leg. "I agree that Vale didn't have the opportunity to go hide his gun somewhere. After I shot him, and he fell to the ground, it must have come loose. The momentum of his fall could have knocked the gun into the woods. That's exactly what happened when you knocked me down. My pistol flew into the bushes."

"True. It did. But only a few yards away. And I ran at you, trying to reach you before you pulled the trigger. I'm a big guy. The force of me hitting you and falling to the ground with you is more force than if Vale simply dropped where he stood after being injured. Don't you agree?"

Reluctantly, she nodded. "Agreed."

"And yet your gun only flew about six feet away. Wouldn't you expect Vale's gun, if he had one, to have gone only a few feet, given that set of parameters? Therefore easily found by either me or the crime scene tech team later?"

She didn't answer. What could she say?

"After taking your gun, I was with Vale the rest of the time. I was there with the medical team. I escorted them down the mountain to the waiting ambulance. At no time did I ever see a gun."

He waited. Again she said nothing.

"This might be a good time to tell the truth," he said.

She was starting to regret apologizing for punching him.

"I *am* telling the truth."

He sat back in his chair. "So the gun just, what, walked away on its own?"

"Maybe Vale threw it."

"Sure. Okay. When he was lying on the ground bleeding out?"

"At any time when he was on the ground when you were on top of me. He could have tossed it away."

"The crime scene techs would have found it."

"Not if they didn't know to look for it. You never spoke to me after the shooting. You didn't ask me why I shot Vale. You didn't know he had a gun, so you wouldn't have told the techs to look for one."

"Valid point. Rangers McAlister and Grady took you into custody before I went down the mountain with the medical team. Did you mention at any time to either of them that you thought Vale had a gun?"

Once again, he found the hole in her argument. She clenched her jaw in frustration. Of course she'd told them that Vale had a gun. She didn't want someone to think that she'd just arbitrarily shot an unarmed man.

"I'll take that as a yes," he continued. "I'll be sure to verify that with the rangers. But I imagine it will be in McAlister's report. He's the one who would have sent the crime scene guys up there, too. And I'm sure he would have told them to perform a thorough search for a second gun. Again, I'll happily verify that when I read their reports. Just to be extra certain, I'll ask them, too. But we both know what they'll say. They looked for a gun. They didn't find one. Again, this would be a really good time to come clean, to dig yourself out of the hole you're getting into."

She shook her head.

"Let's start again with why you're here."

"I told you. I'm hiking."

"In the winter."

"In the winter," she snapped.

His brows rose. "Okay. So you like the cold. You like treacherous, slippery trails with snow and ice. Not my thing. But I can see the appeal for some people. The mountains are definitely beautiful with their snowcaps."

He was going somewhere with this. She decided not to help him by rising to the bait. She sat back and waited.

"So you're out hiking, enjoying the frigid weather. You heard someone else on the trail, behind you, so you—a trained FBI agent—whirled around and shot him. Do I have that right?"

"I told him to freeze. He didn't."

"Right. Left that part out. You heard someone behind you, whirled around, yelled for him to freeze, then you pulled the trigger."

"After he pulled a gun out of his pocket, yes."

"Because you thought he was walking on the same trail as you? You assumed he was following you?"

"Yes. No." She shook her head in frustration. "It's more complicated than that."

He rested his forearms on the table again. "I'm all ears."

She really, really wanted to punch him. "He wasn't

simply following me. He was *stalking* me through the woods, for quite some time. At least half an hour."

His brows rose. "Stalking you?"

"Hunting me. Matching me stride for stride. When I took a step, he'd take a step, echoing me so that it was difficult to be sure if someone else was out there, following me."

"Following you."

"Would you quit repeating everything I say?"

He held up his hands in a placating gesture. "How long have you known Kurt Vale?"

"Known him? I've never met him."

"But he's been stalking you. I think you used the word *hunting*."

"Yes. Exactly. He was hunting me. That's how it seemed. I could hear footsteps—"

"Echoing yours."

"You're being condescending."

"My apologies."

He wasn't sincere and they both knew it. He was tripping her up, making what had happened seem... trivial. She tried again to explain. "I was scared, okay? I believed he was after me."

"Why would he be after you if he didn't know you?"

"Because..." She hesitated. Would he believe her if she told him? Things weren't going so well. If she was on a jury listening in on this conversation right now, she'd lock herself up and throw away the key. Duncan certainly didn't believe her. That was obvious. He wasn't likely to believe her *wild theories*, either, as her boss in Denver called them. Instead of telling Duncan her latest theory, her reason for being here, she tried again to stick to the facts of what had happened. What she needed to do was make him understand her fear, that she'd felt threatened. She would never shoot someone otherwise. She wasn't a cold-blooded murderer.

"You're a man," she said. "An intimidating one, sizewise, especially to a woman who is half your height, like me."

He smiled. "Half might be stretching it."

He was back to playing good cop, trying to charm and disarm her with those smiles of his. She cleared her throat. "My point is that even though I'm trained in self-defense, I know my physical limitations. I had a gun with me for protection—"

"You expected that you might end up in a confrontation and need your weapon?"

She'd not only expected it. She'd hoped for it. But telling him that would seal her fate.

"Hope for the best, prepare for the worst. I took my gun with me just in case. This morning, when I was walking the trail, I heard sounds—"

"Sounds?"

"Rocks pinging against other rocks, like someone's feet had accidentally kicked them. A coat or jacket brushing against a tree."

"The sounds any hiker might make while heading down a trail."

"No, no, you don't understand."

"I want to." He leaned forward, his dark blue eyes

watching her with an intensity that was unnerving.
"Make me understand, Remi. Tell me the truth."

She could practically hear Jack Nicholson yelling,
"You can't handle the truth," his famous line from
A Few Good Men. Hysterical laughter bubbled up
in her throat. She forced it down, drew several long,
deep breaths.

"The sounds I heard weren't loud or obvious. They
were…stealthy. Like someone was trying to be quiet.
It was difficult to pinpoint the direction. But someone
was definitely following me. Not hiking, like I was.
They were actually specifically following me. I'm
absolutely one hundred percent certain." This time
she was the one to lean forward, her gaze clashing
with his. "I tested my theory. Every once in a while
I'd stop, with my foot in the air instead of taking my
next step. I heard him, a thump in the distance, as if
he was walking in sync with me, using my footsteps
to hide the sound of his. But when I stopped suddenly, in midstride, he couldn't. That's when I knew
for sure. Do you understand?"

He didn't say anything. He didn't have to. The
skeptical look on his face said it all.

They watched each other for a full minute before
he leaned back again. "Let's see if I have this right.
You were scared."

"Yes."

"Someone was following you."

"Yes."

"You were convinced they were stalking you."

"Yes."

"That they intended you harm."

"Definitely."

"How long were they following you?"

"At least half an hour."

"At what point did you call the police, knowing someone was following you, stalking you, someone you felt wanted to do you harm? When did you call?" He looked down at his keyboard, as if ready to record the time.

She stared at him, feeling the trap closing around her. She hadn't even seen it coming.

He looked up, feigning surprise. "What time did you call the police during this half hour that you felt your life was in danger?"

Her left hand went reflexively to her cell phone, which McAlister had returned to her and which was now in her jeans pocket. "I didn't call anyone."

"You didn't?"

"No. I didn't."

"Really? Why not?"

"Cell phone service?" she blurted out. "No signal?"

"Are those questions or statements?"

She pursed her lips.

"Are you stating, on the record and on camera, that you tried to call, but couldn't get a signal?"

Her mouth went dry. She'd made a guess about lack of cell phone service and didn't have a clue whether or not she could have gotten a call through. But she would bet that *he* did. He probably knew where every cell tower was in these mountains, where you could get a signal and where you couldn't. Technically, she hadn't outright lied yet. She hadn't specifically said that she'd looked at her phone and saw no bars. But if she told him she'd tried to call, she'd be crossing that line. She'd be lying to a federal officer in the course of an investigation, a crime that alone could send her to prison and destroy her career, if it wasn't destroyed already.

"No." Her voice came out as a dry croak. She cleared her throat, then reached for the bottle of water and took a long swallow.

He waited until she'd finished and set the bottle down. "No, you didn't have a signal, or no, you didn't attempt to call for help?"

Good grief. He was like a fox after a rabbit.

"I'm a law-enforcement officer," she said. "I had a gun for protection, if I needed it. Although I was afraid, and worried that someone was after me, I felt confident in my ability to protect myself."

"Did you call the police?"

"No. I did not."

He smiled. "That wasn't so hard, was it? You told the truth. Cell coverage is spotty and unreliable throughout the park. That's why we carry radios. But there's a cell tower not far from here that provides excellent signal strength. You would have easily gotten a call out if you'd tried."

She pressed her left hand to her stomach. It felt like a kaleidoscope of butterflies was fluttering around inside her. Or a swarm. Or whatever a gazillion butterflies was called.

His smile faded. "Of course that brings us back to the original question of why you didn't try to call anyone. Using your own logic, if you were thinking like a law-enforcement officer, using your training, you would know to call for backup. Standard operating procedure when you're in danger. Why didn't you call?"

She didn't answer.

"You truly believed that Mr. Vale was coming after you?"

"Yes," she whispered.

"Then why, when you could have called for backup, did you choose to risk your life and face him all alone?"

Because I wanted to catch the bastard myself.

She pressed her lips together to keep from blurting out those very words.

Silence filled the room. He stretched his long legs out in front of him and let out a deep sigh.

"I was the first one at the office this morning," he said. "I was the only one here when Zack Towers called to report that he'd shared one of the shelters on the Appalachian Trail last night with another hiker. When you left, you must have put your hand in your pocket to check your gun. He saw the outline of the pistol and called it in. No guns are allowed in any national park unless you're one of the rangers or investigators working for the National Park Service. That rules you out."

Her shoulder was beginning to throb from sitting in one position so long. She rubbed it to ease the ache.

"There was a hiker with me in the shelter last night. I don't remember him being named Zack, though. I thought his name was Sunny."

Duncan nodded. "Sunny's his trail name. He's one of our regulars around here, shows up every year around this time, one of the few who likes to hike the AT during the winter. He's a section hiker."

"Section hiker?"

"Since you're out here hiking the Appalachian Trail, I assumed you would have studied up on the lingo." He let his words hang in the air between them.

Wearying of his game, she said, "I'm only doing day hikes. Normally, I stay in the motel each night and come back in the morning. I don't know all the terminology because, obviously, I'm not one of those people who can miraculously afford to dedicate nearly a year of their lives to become a two-thousand-miler. That is what they call people who hike from Georgia to Maine in one season, right? NOBOs are the northbound hikers. SOBOs are the southbound ones?"

He nodded. "Sounds like you studied a little bit about the AT before coming here. I wonder why you'd do that? Maybe because you wanted to make sure there wouldn't be a lot of hiker traffic around to see whatever it is that you're actually doing here?"

"Or maybe I learned way more than I ever wanted to know about this cursed place when I was here on a stupid senior trip back in high school," she snapped.

His look of surprise had her closing her own eyes and cursing to herself. She was getting too stirred up, too frustrated. And as a result, she'd just told him something way too close to her true purpose in being here.

The sound of him typing had her opening her eyes.

He typed a moment longer, then looked at her over the top of the screen. "What's your natural hair color?"

She blinked. "Excuse me?"

"Your eyebrows are dark. You're a brunette, right?"

"And this matters why?"

He turned the laptop around so she could see the screen. There, in living color, smiling and looking carefree, was her sister in the picture her father had given to the police when Becca went missing. It was the picture from the flyer they'd circulated by the hundreds in Gatlinburg after she disappeared. It was the same picture he'd put on the website he'd created to try to generate leads that would help him find his daughter. But they never did.

Becca.

Her throat tight, she whispered, "Why are you doing this? What do you want from me?"

Something flashed in his eyes. Sorrow? Regret? Empathy? Whatever it was, it didn't bother him enough to close the laptop, or minimize the picture of her sister. Instead, his gaze searched hers.

"What I want is what I've wanted all along—the truth. I want you to admit that you came here because your boss, and the Behavioral Analysis Unit, refused to believe your theories about serial killers. I think that you dyed your hair blond to make yourself fit the criteria for whatever serial killer you're currently theorizing about. And I think you very nearly killed Kurt Vale because you mistakenly thought that he was that killer." He tapped the screen, drawing her attention to her sister's picture again. "So, tell me, Remi. What's the current theory? What killer are you after? If I hadn't stopped you, would you have murdered Vale because you believe he killed your sister?"

She swore a string of obscenities at him and shoved herself up from her chair. She threw a few more insults out into the universe for good measure, then stalked out of the room.

Chapter Six

Duncan plopped his legs on top of his desk and grabbed a red apple out of his snack drawer. "Shouldn't Lee and Grady be back with lunch by now?" he complained around a mouthful of the sweet, juicy apple. "I'm starving."

McAlister stood beside Duncan's desk, looking out the front window. "What do you think she's doing?" He motioned toward Remi as she stalked back and forth in the gravel parking lot, golden hair bouncing around her shoulders, cell phone glued to her ear.

Duncan shrugged. "As red as her face is, she's probably yelling at Supervisory Special Agent Johnson for emailing a copy of her personnel file to us. Or she's freezing. Or both. When she calms down she'll realize she left her jacket in here."

"Maybe I should take it to her." In four steps, McAlister had the puffy white coat in his hand, ready to play the chivalrous knight to their fuming guest.

"Don't," Duncan said. "She has more incentive to come back inside on her own if she's shivering."

McAlister dropped the jacket on top of Duncan's

outstretched legs and braced his hand on the wall beside the window. "You don't seem worried that she'll take off."

"Where's she gonna go?" He frowned at a large bruise on the apple and turned it, looking for a better spot. "She doesn't have her car up here. She's injured. No backpack of supplies. No jacket. I'll bet you dinner that she won't last five more minutes outside." He took another bite.

"I think you just bought me dinner."

Duncan glanced up. Remi wasn't on the phone anymore. She was running, fast, across the gravel, heading away from the trailer. She was already halfway to the road. "Ah, hell."

McAlister started laughing.

Duncan tossed the rest of the apple in the trash and grabbed Remi's coat.

"I'm thinking a big medium-rare steak will do the trick," McAlister called after him as he ran for the door. "One of those delicious fill-it mig-non numbers at The Peddler Steakhouse. Or maybe a New York strip."

"Rain check," Duncan yelled, grabbing his jacket and gloves before barreling outside. He cleared the concrete steps in one leap and landed with a bone-jarring crunch on the gravel.

Remi was nowhere to be seen.

The door opened behind him and McAlister leaned out. "Looks like she's headed to town. She turned left at the road."

"Thanks, Pops!" Duncan sprinted after her, yanking on his gloves and jacket as he went.

Five minutes later he was back at his Jeep, cursing as he hopped inside and tossed Remi's coat on the seat beside him. How a woman a hair over five feet tall could outrun his long stride was beyond him. He would have caught up to her eventually, but closing the gap between them had been taking far too long.

He peeled out of the parking lot, adding a few new gravel dents to the metal storage shed that housed their ATVs and snowplow attachments.

It didn't take long to catch up to her in the Jeep. She was running on the shoulder of the road at a ground-eating pace. As he slowed alongside her, he rolled down the passenger window.

"Need a lift, pretty lady?" he drawled.

The tightening of her mouth was the only sign that she'd heard him. She stared straight ahead, her hair whipping behind her. Something about her stride seemed off. It dawned on him that it was because of her hurt shoulder. She was using her left hand to hold the sling, probably so it wouldn't bounce against her chest as she ran. Judging by the lines of pain bracketing the side of her mouth, it wasn't working very well.

The cold made her cheeks ruddy. But the rest of her face, and her arms, were even paler than before. Apparently, he'd goaded her enough that she was willing to cause herself pain rather than answer more of his questions.

Someone give him an award. He was officially the biggest jerk on the planet.

"I'm sorry," he called to her through the open window, careful to keep the Jeep a safe distance away in case he hit a patch of ice. "Did you hear me?"

"I heard you," she bit out.

"And?"

Her jaw tightened. "What are you apologizing for?"

"For doing my job?"

"Wrong answer." She still wouldn't look at him.

"And for using personal information in an unintentionally mean way to try to break you down so you'd tell me the truth."

"Unintentional? Seriously?"

"I wasn't trying to *hurt* you, Remi. I was using the tools I had to make you answer my questions. I realize now I might have gone too far. And I really am sorry about that."

She glanced at him, looking more surprised than angry now.

"To be fair," he added, "I was doing it for your own good."

Her look turned incredulous. "For my own good? Using the tragedy of my sister's disappearance to *break* me was for my own good?" *Crunch, crunch, crunch.* Her boots kept rhythm in the snow on the road's shoulder.

"I ran track and field at the University of Tennessee," he said. "I'll bet you could beat half the guys on my team. How fast can you do a mile if you go all out?"

"First, UT, the Big Orange, really? Second, let's skip the small talk. I'm not your friend, Duncan McKenzie."

"You could be. If you wanted. And what's wrong with UT?"

"Buffaloes beat fruit any day of the week."

"University of Colorado?"

She nodded.

"At UT, we're known as humanitarians, you know, the Tennessee Vols, or volunteers. Orange is our color. Not our fruit."

"Whatever. You've got a dog as your mascot. A big, powerful buffalo trumps that."

"Smokey's a bluetick coonhound. I bet he'd nip at the heels of Ralphie the Buffalo and send him running for cover."

She rolled her eyes.

Neither of them spoke as they rounded a curve. When they were on a straightaway again, he said, "I do want to help you—even if you are a CU Buff." When she didn't respond to his teasing, he added, "I don't want to put a fellow law-enforcement officer in jail—as long as you can give me a plausible explanation behind the shooting. You definitely aren't telling me the whole story. And I suspect what you aren't telling me has to do with your sister. Am I right?"

Crunch, crunch, crunch.

"Okay. I could be wrong about that," he allowed. "I'm still open to an explanation that will make sense of what happened. There has to be more to the story. You don't strike me as a cold-blooded killer or even the reckless-endangerment type."

"Gee, thanks for that resounding vote of confidence."

"Give me some leeway here. We didn't exactly meet under the best of circumstances. If you were in my position, wouldn't you be suspicious? At least to start off?"

Thump, crunch, thump. There wasn't much snow in this section of the road. They slowly turned another curve, then straightened out.

"I guess so," she relented.

"All right. Let's work with that. I'm an investigator, like you. Just doing my job. Clay and I are buds, but I need facts to back up my recommendations about possible charges."

"Clay?"

"Clay Perry, the district attorney. He's a Vols grad, too."

"Oh goody."

He grinned, then sobered. "It's in your best interest to talk to me, Remi. You need to tell me all of it, the whole truth, or I won't be able to keep you out of jail."

When she didn't say anything, he added, "Be honest. You're more angry at your boss than at me. He's the one who shared your personnel file with Johnson, who shared it with my boss, who shared it with me. I'm just the little guppy in the big pond here."

She stumbled, then straightened. "He shared my personnel file with you?"

Well, dang. Maybe he shouldn't have mentioned that little piece of information. "I thought you figured that out. Wasn't he the one you were shouting at on the phone?"

"Yes. But I just thought he *told* you about my background, my family tragedy. I didn't know he shared... everything."

"I guess the possum's out of the sack now. My bad. I shouldn't have told you that."

"Possum? Never mind. Must be a Tennessee thing."

"Actually, I think it's a McKenzie thing."

Her lips twitched, then thinned.

"I saw that. Made you smile."

"It happens. Don't take it personally."

"You wound me deeply, bonny lass." He used his best Irish accent. But instead of laughing, she turned her head and looked straight at him with a somber expression. The bleakness in her eyes sent a pang straight to his heart.

"You hurt me," she accused.

"I know." He cleared his throat. "I know, and I'm sorry. I really am."

"But you'd do it all over again?"

He started to tell her no, but then thought about it and shook his head. "Honestly, I probably would."

She said something beneath her breath that no doubt would have burned his ears if he'd caught the words.

"If I did have the chance for a do-over," he said, "I'd lock the conference room door so you couldn't run off. And I'd feel awful later for doing it. That's how I feel right now. Like a big fat donkey with long ears and a furry butt."

A choked sound escaped her. She cleared her throat and kept running.

"Come on, Remi. Even your goose bumps are getting goose bumps." He held up her jacket. "It's warm and toasty in the Jeep."

Her gaze shot longingly to the jacket. She slowed to a jog.

He slowed the Jeep.

She stopped.

He swore as he drove past her, then stopped and backed up.

She rested her left arm on the door. "I'm not going back in that interrogation room without a lawyer."

He groaned. "My boss will be thrilled. But I suppose I earned that. If you won't talk to me, though, I'll have to lock you up. You're still under arrest, still in my custody. And with nothing to give the DA, that's where you'll remain."

Her brow furrowed. "You're not playing fair."

"You're the one threatening me with a lawyer." He shivered dramatically.

Her lips twitched again, then she gave in to the impulse and smiled. "I like you, Duncan McKenzie. You're handsome and funny when you aren't being a bully."

He grinned. "Am I blushing? 'Cause I feel like I'm blushing."

"Shut up." She fumbled with the door handle.

"Hold on. You can't climb up in this thing with that shoulder." He jumped down and had just reached the passenger door when she hopped up inside.

She arched a brow. "Look, Pa. I did it all by myself."

"Are you always this stubborn?" He stood in the V

of the open door, grabbed the seat belt before she could and gently pulled it over her shoulder.

As he clicked the buckle into place, she said, "I don't like to feel helpless."

He lifted his head, still half inside the truck with his hand on the seat belt, dangerously close to her hip. Her eyes widened. But he didn't pull away. Instead, he met her gaze, all teasing gone.

"I'm so sorry about your sister," he said. "I've got three brothers and am blessed to still have both of my parents around. Losing one of them—even my black sheep baby brother, who causes more pain than joy in our family—would, well, it would probably destroy me. The fact that you've survived, and built your life around seeking justice for others in spite of your pain, is humbling and amazing. I'm honestly, truly sorry for your loss and that I hurt you."

Her eyes seemed overbright, as if she was fighting back tears. "Thank you," she whispered.

"Remi?"

She sniffed. "Yes?"

"Sometimes you have to take a leap of faith in life. I think this may be your time to take that leap."

Her brow wrinkled. "What do you mean?"

"I like you. And not just because you're gorgeous."

Her eyes looked like big moons as she blinked at him.

"I want to help you," he said. "Because you seem like a good, decent person. You've been dealt some tough cards that aren't your fault. As a result, you got yourself in an untenable situation. But you have to trust me and help me to help you."

"Are you trying to talk me out of getting a lawyer?"

He chuckled. "No. But that would be a nice boon. I admit it."

"Then what are you asking?"

He sighed and backed away to a safer distance. She was way too beautiful, and tempting, up close. Something he'd been able to mostly ignore before now. But somewhere in the past few minutes they'd crossed the line from interrogator and suspect to... something else. He needed to be careful in how he proceeded, at least until he figured out the dynamics going on between them.

Resting his arm on the roof above the door opening, he said, "I'm saying that a burden is easier to bear if you share it. From what I read in your file, and knowing that both your real boss and your pseudoboss threw you under the bus by sharing your personnel file with us, I can imagine that you've felt isolated at work for a long time. And since you haven't asked to be allowed to call a boyfriend or even a friend all day, I'm guessing you're alone in your private life, too."

She stiffened. "That's none of your business. And you're veering back into being-a-jerk territory again."

"Maybe so. I guess I'm rusty at being a friend. Being a workaholic, I don't have a girlfriend at the moment, either, in case you're wondering." He winked. "Between the job and family, I don't get out much these days."

"I can't tell if you're trying to explain your behavior or whether you're hitting on me."

He winced. "Did I really sound that smarmy?"

She nodded.

"My bad." He held up his hands in a placating gesture. "I admit, you're beautiful and funny when you aren't punching me. But I really am offering an olive branch here."

She rolled her eyes, then seemed to reluctantly grin. "Am I blushing? 'Cause I feel like I'm blushing."

He chuckled. "Did we just make a truce?"

She grew serious. "No."

He sighed with disappointment. "Ah, well. I figured it might be too much to ask. It's too soon. I'll try again later."

She laughed. "You're impossible. I think we just became friends. That's way better than a truce."

"Friends. Sounds good." He shut the door and hurried to the driver's side. After getting in and buckling his seat belt, he said, "Friendship or not, I still have a job to do. I have to take you back until the matter of charges, or no charges, is settled."

He turned the Jeep around and headed up the mountain. "Do you have a specific lawyer in mind?"

"Never needed one before. I don't exactly have one on speed dial."

"Speaking off the record, as a friend, I can make a few calls. My dad's known as Mighty McKenzie, a retired federal judge who has the reputation of a bulldog when it comes to getting justice. Mom's a former prosecutor and can hold her own against anyone, too.

Between the both of them, I'm sure they know someone to recommend."

"Duncan?"

"Hmm?"

"It looks like there's a road up ahead on the left.
Could you pull in there, please?"

He looked where she was pointing. "That's an old
bird-watching trail, not really a road anymore. The
underbrush grew up too thick around it and we don't
maintain it. Plus, it leads to an abandoned farmhouse
that's ready to slide off the edge of a cliff. It's off-
limits."

"I didn't say drive down the whole length of the
road. Just pull in a little out of the way and park. I'm
pretty sure this four-wheel drive Jeep can handle it,
aren't you?"

He looked at her in question.

"I'm asking as a friend," she said. "Take a leap of
faith for me."

He grinned and gave her his best *Back to the
Future* Doc Brown impression. "Road, who needs
roads?"

Her lips twitched, telling him she'd gotten his
vague paraphrased classic movie reference. Which
definitely had him liking her more. Maybe he'd test
her *Guardians of the Galaxy* knowledge sometime.

"All right," he said. "Hold on. This *leap* is going
to jar your shoulder."

"I ran all the way here. A few more bumps aren't
going to make much of a difference."

He slowed and then turned onto the narrow trail.

As predicted, the Jeep bounced around, even though he was being as careful as possible. Branches scraped the roof, then the sides. His boss was going to love how he was treating government property. A new paint job might be in the Jeep's immediate future. But he was more worried about how the bouncing might impact Remi. He winced after hitting a particularly rough spot, and looked at her.

"That's far enough." Her voice was raw, her posture stiff as she held on to her hurt arm. "Stop so we can talk."

He put the Jeep in Park and turned to face her. "Okay. I leaped. What do you want to talk about?"

"I don't want a lawyer."

"O…kay."

"What you said back there, in the conference room, right before I stormed out, is very close to the truth."

He frowned. He'd said a lot of things. "Which part?"

"You read my whole personnel file?"

"Every word." Twice.

"Then you know that I joined the FBI with the intention of becoming a member of the Behavioral Analysis Unit one day, although that hasn't happened yet. I wanted to learn how to profile and capture the worst types of killers out there, serial killers."

"Because you think your sister was…taken…by a serial killer?"

"Not exactly. I don't have any evidence that points to that. But I figured if I studied with the best and brightest investigative minds out there, it would eventually help me in my personal quest to discover who took my sister. And if I could put away some really terrible monsters along the way, it was a win-win."

"But that's not what happened."

"No," she said. "It isn't. To be fair to my boss, he's right that my sister's disappearance is an obsession for me. It influences, informs, every decision I make, and it has cast a shadow over my entire career. I've read my sister's case file dozens of times, social-media stalked Billy Hendricks and Garrett Weber—the two most likely suspects. But nothing ever came of it, no new information, nothing to point to the guilt of either of them. So I've poured my energies into other crimes, other victims, other suspects. I've come up with some pretty crazy theories over the years, thinking I've tracked down patterns that indicate killers are operating in a specific area. And I've brought those theories to my boss and the BAU. They listened to me the first few times I went to them. They even dug around, looked into my claims. But I was new, made a lot of mistakes and my theories were disproved."

"Every time?"

"Every time."

The pain in her voice had him reaching for her hand without even thinking about it. Her eyes widening was what made him look down and realize that he'd laced their fingers together. Even with his gloves on, it felt so right that he didn't let go. Neither did she.

"Go on," he said, surprised at how good it felt to

hold her hand. "You were saying that your theories were always wrong."

"Yes." Her voice sounded hoarse. She coughed. "I, ah, came up with a new theory about six months ago that I've been working on. But this one I haven't told anyone about. I wanted to be sure first. I've cried wolf too many times in the past. No one takes me seriously. So I decided to do something about it on my own, to try to get some kind of proof before going to the BAU again."

"Am I right in thinking that dyeing your hair was part of that search for proof?"

"I bleached it because the man I'm after abducts and presumably kills women who have straight blond hair and are in their midtwenties. I'm twenty-seven and figured that sacrificing my brown locks to match his preferred-victim characteristics was a small price to pay to get this man off the streets. Or out of the woods, I suppose. I believe he's targeting women in national parks, like this one. I've examined hundreds of missing persons cases to arrive at my theory."

"So you thought it was a good idea to come here and offer yourself as bait."

She winced and tugged her hand free from his. He belatedly realized he'd been squeezing too tightly.

"Sorry," he said. "I'm having a hard time wrapping my mind around the fact that you would put yourself in harm's way like that. With no backup. If I hadn't been there, if Vale had been the killer and he'd managed to sneak up on you without you hearing him, things could have gone very differently this morning."

"What makes you so sure that he isn't the killer? You haven't even heard my theory."

"Well, for one thing, he didn't have a gun."

She narrowed her eyes in warning.

"Okay, okay," he said. "Maybe his gun, knives, rope, duct tape and the rest of his serial killer torture implements were hidden away in a go-bag that he didn't have on him at the time. Maybe he keeps his go-bag in his car, like I keep mine in my Jeep, minus the torture implements, of course. Go ahead. I'm all ears. What's the theory?"

"If you're going to make fun of me, I won't bother. I can get that kind of treatment from my boss any day of the week."

"Ouch. All right. I'll be good. Go on. Tell me about your research."

She hesitated, as if weighing whether or not to trust him. Then she let out a long breath. "I need a piece of paper."

"How very old-fashioned of you." He popped the glove box open and dug around inside. "Fresh out of paper. How about a napkin?"

"That'll work."

He set a napkin on the seat between them and closed the glove box.

"Pen?" She held her hand out expectantly.

"Oh, right." He rummaged around in a pile of change in a cup holder and extracted a pen. "Here you go. It might be a bit sticky. I spilled some coffee in there this morning and haven't had a chance to clean it."

She grimaced and turned the pen, apparently to a less sticky spot. Then she drew a series of dots on the napkin, seven in all, and connected them with lines. She held it up to him. "What does that look like?"

He tilted his head, studying the drawing. "Is this one of those sexual harassment things? It kinda seems inappropriate, unless this is a friends thing instead of agent-to-agent stuff."

Her eyes widened. "What?" She turned the napkin toward her. "No. I don't even…no. It's a unicorn. Don't you see it?" She flipped it around again.

He stared at the dots and lines and gave up. "I'm guessing you didn't win any art awards in school."

She dropped the napkin to her lap. "I'm being serious."

"So am I. That doesn't look like a unicorn."

She plopped the napkin on the seat between them. "The Big Dipper doesn't look like an actual dipper, either. Not really. You have to use your imagination. In your case, maybe you should borrow some of mine, since you apparently don't have one."

"This is us being friends again, right? Insulting each other? It's fun. I don't know why I don't have more friends."

"I do," she grumbled.

He grinned.

She tapped the drawing. "The horse—"

"Unicorn."

"The *unicorn* is facing to the right. It's in profile. That's why there are only two legs. This is the horn." She ran a fingernail between two of the dots.

"These are the withers—the shoulders, basically."
She pointed to the other lines and named the various parts. "It's a constellation. It's called Monoceros now. When it was first discovered, the full name was Monoceros Unicornis."

"If you say so. What does that have to do with women going missing?"

"Each star represents a specific geographical location where a woman disappeared. When I superimpose the constellation over a map of the southeast section of the United States, the points line up."

The Jeep shook. They both looked up. Leaves fluttered on the bushes by the trail. Farther down, tree branches swayed up and down in the wind, like a crowd doing the wave at a football game. The sky was darkening overhead. But it was far too early for the sun to be going down.

"The weather guys have been warning about a storm all week. Looks like it's finally starting to roll in," he said. "I reckon we've got a couple hours of clear skies left. But up here the temps will start dropping long before that. We should head back to base."

She let out a sigh. "All right. Maybe Pops has an archaic pad of paper I can use. It'll work better than a napkin."

He smiled. "Knowing Pops, I imagine he does. The man keeps printouts of every case our team has ever worked on. He's responsible for half the stuff we have in storage."

He put the Jeep in Reverse, since there wasn't any room to turn around. He'd just backed onto the road when his phone buzzed. After checking his mirrors to make sure that no one was heading up the road behind them, Duncan looked at the screen. It was his boss. He'd likely passed right by them while they were parked on the trail. He and Pup were probably at the trailer, wondering where he was, and where Remi was. He should have called Pops and let him know that he'd found her, safe and sound.

He answered the call. "Hey, Lee. I've got Remi with me and—"

His boss interrupted him, and made a startling announcement. Duncan's gaze flew to Remi, his stomach dropping as if he'd just gone downhill on a steep roller coaster. "All right," he said when Lee finished. "We're on our way." He ended the call and punched the gas, sending the Jeep racing up the road.

"Duncan? What's wrong? What's going on?"

"You said you've been looking at cases where women went missing in national parks, plural. But you chose this particular park when you tried to bait the killer. Why?"

"That's what I was showing you earlier. It's all about the constellation and how it lines up with the various locations."

"Explain it to me."

"We just missed our turn. The trailer was back there."

"I'm taking you up the mountain, back to the gap where we were this morning."

"I don't understand. I thought it was dangerous. A storm is blowing in."

"That was Lee on the phone. He just got a call about a missing hiker, in the same area you were in this morning. The hiker's a woman in her midtwenties with long blond hair." He glanced at her horrified expression and immediately regretted his lack of finesse with his announcement.

"She hasn't been gone long," he said, trying to reassure her. "People do get lost up here a lot. It doesn't mean anything nefarious is going on. But the coincidence is too strong to ignore. If there's even a chance that her disappearance is connected to your theory, then I need to know everything you can tell me about your research. Right now."

Chapter Seven

Remi awkwardly reached her left arm across her lap and grabbed the armrest as Duncan's Jeep careened around a curve. If it weren't for her seat belt she'd be pinging around the interior like a pinball. As it was, her right shoulder kept bumping the door enough to have her biting the inside of her cheek and tasting blood.

Another turn and he had to slam his brakes to keep from ramming into the back of a long-bed pickup truck with a pair of ATVs bouncing around in the back.

"Pops never did learn how to drive over the speed limit," he complained, riding so close to the truck in front of them that Remi wanted to scream.

"How did you know a woman would go missing here? How did you know it would happen today?" he asked.

"I didn't."

He shot her an aggravated look. "I thought we were being honest with each other. A woman's life could be on the line."

"Don't you think I know that? I'm not lying." She definitely preferred the grinning, playful Duncan over this serious, all-business side.

He slammed the brakes again, narrowly missing Pops's bumper as the man maneuvered around a dip in the road. She grabbed the handle above the door window to keep from being thrown around. "Good grief, would you slow down before you get us killed?"

Surprisingly, he did. Not by much, but enough so that her insides no longer felt like they were rattling against her ribs.

"Your latest theory," he urged again, his voice laced with impatience. "The woman who disappeared is Sheryl Foster. She's got a husband and two small children. If you know anything that might help us find her, I need to hear it."

Her heart sank. "I wish... I don't..." She clutched the handle above her harder. "I wish I could help. But I'm not a criminal profiler. And I haven't run across anything yet that gives me a clue about the identity of whoever is behind these abductions. Offering myself as a potential victim was my big plan to draw him out. I've got nothing else."

"There are seven dots on that map. Different parks, right?"

"Different parks."

"Why did you come to this one? Why didn't you choose one of the others?"

"Because he'd already hit the other parks. This was the last one to make the constellation complete."

"The seventh dot?"

"Yes."

He seemed to consider that a moment. "What about the timing? How did you know he'd strike today?"

"I believed he'd strike this month, not today specifically. The unicorn constellation is only visible during February. The stars are very faint. You'd have to know something about astronomy to even know to look for it, and of course have a good telescope."

"You're an astronomy expert?"

"Not really. But I know more than the average person, by osmosis. My twin sister, Becca, she was totally into it. Had tons of books on the subject, telescopes. Every school project from elementary school on was about planets and stars and wormholes. Half her clothes either had a picture of a star on them or some kind of scientific fact about the stars." She waved her hand as if waving away her words. "My point is, we were really close, and shared a bedroom most of our lives. Whether I wanted to or not, I ended up learning about this stuff."

"Five minutes." He jerked the wheel to keep them from bouncing into a ditch.

Remi's pulse slammed in her throat. She half expected them to slide off the road at the next curve and barrel into a tree. She swallowed and kept her gaze on Duncan rather than the rocks and trees rushing past them in a blur. Pops was definitely going over the speed limit now. Probably because he was terrified that the tailgater behind him was going to ram his truck.

"Thoughts of Becca are never far from my mind.

She disappeared here, in this park, over a decade ago. So when I began working for the FBI and started my own research on the side, I focused on murders and disappearances in the Smokies. It spiraled out from there."

"You think this guy is the same one who abducted your twin?"

"No, actually, I don't. The victimology is all wrong. She was much younger than the other women. And she had shoulder-length curly brown hair, like me. At least, when I'm not in bait mode and styling or dyeing my hair accordingly."

His gaze shot to hers again. "Please tell me you haven't done this before, changed your looks and paraded yourself in some remote area, purposely offering yourself up as bait for a killer."

She chewed her bottom lip.

He swore.

She drew a bracing breath. "Like I said, because of Becca, I tend to focus on missing persons cases in national parks. I'm hoping one day I'll stumble onto something that will help me solve her disappearance. But in the meantime, I started noticing disappearances of young blond Caucasian women, always the same time of year, in February. I plotted them out on a map. That's when I saw the pattern."

He still seemed to be upset over her baiting killers. His jaw was clenched so tight the skin had gone white. Remi sensed that his anger wasn't directed *at* her, it was on her behalf. He was concerned about her safety. She couldn't fault him for that. And couldn't deny that it felt good that one person in this world actually cared, even if only because he was a decent guy and would care about anyone putting themselves in harm's way. She could pretend it was because she was special to him, an actual friend. It felt too good not to try to hold on to that feeling, at least for a little while.

His deep voice broke into her thoughts. "The pattern you saw, it was the unicorn in the stars?"

She nodded, but since he wasn't looking at her she added, "Yes. There were six points, only one left to make the pattern complete. Six data points isn't much to pin a theory on, especially when the constellation in question isn't one that most people have ever heard of. I mean, what are the odds of some serial killer out there being a star nut like my sister and even knowing about Monoceros? The only reason I knew about it was because Becca loved unicorns and had a picture of Monoceros on our bedroom wall. But I couldn't shake the coincidence that the constellation is only viewable in February, and all of these women went missing in February. I figured if my theory was right, he would definitely strike here this month. So I took vacation, and took a chance."

Her throat felt tight as she admitted, "I should have told you all of this as soon as I was arrested. Instead, I sat there trying to protect myself and hoping you'd let me go so I could go back on the ridge. If I'd told you, maybe you could have—"

"What? Evacuated half a million acres? Warned all blond women to stay away from the Smoky Mountains for the entire month of February?"

"When you put it that way, it does sound ludicrous."

"A few years ago," he said, "we had out-of-control wildfires raging through this area. We blocked off roads and issued warnings on TV, radio, handed out flyers, you name it. People still went into the mountains." He glanced at her. "Trust me, Remi. This isn't something for you to feel guilty about. The only person who owns that guilt is the man who abducted Mrs. Foster—if she was even abducted. She may just be lost. And if she is, we'll find her. All right?"

She nodded and forced a smile. His words did make her feel better. But they didn't completely erase her guilt and unease. All she could do was hope and pray that the missing woman really was lost, and that the rangers would find her quickly, before the storm made them put their search on hold.

Duncan wrestled the Jeep over another bumpy section of road. "Back to your theory. Did the seven stars exactly correspond to the national park locations?"

"You mean was everything to scale, right? Like a million miles between stars equals one hundred miles between abduction sites?"

"Something like that."

"Not at all. I admit I played loosey-goosey when drawing the lines on my map to correspond to the constellation. It was an approximation, not exact science. Which was yet another reason I didn't feel comfortable going to the BAU just yet."

"Then I'm still not following how you decided the killer would strike here. There are four hundred eighteen national park sites in this country. Dozens of them could work with that map you drew."

"True, but those four hundred eighteen sites include monuments, battlefields, forts and half-a-dozen other subcategories. While only sixty include National Park in their name, and are what most people think of when they envision a national park—namely that it's a huge area of land set aside for conservation and recreation. Most, but not all, include mountains, too, and rivers, streams, waterfalls, or in the case of Florida, beaches. All of the women disappeared in one of those sixty official national parks. And only one of those sixty locations could complete that constellation pattern. This one, the Great Smoky Mountains National Park. It was either here, or my theory would be disproven. Honestly, I expected it *would* be disproven. I don't exactly have a great batting average where theories are concerned."

"It may still not pan out."

She nodded, but she had a feeling that he didn't believe that any more than she did. Her gut was telling her that she'd finally stumbled onto a theory that matched reality, and that Sheryl Foster was in a world of trouble right now.

He was silent for a moment, as if he was weighing everything she'd said. If he was her boss, he'd throw her a few eye rolls right about now. Then he'd give her the usual *stick to the work you're paid to do* lecture. Her rote reply, that she was doing this research on her own time, never gained her any brownie points. If anything, she lost them, because he'd prefer that, if she wanted to go above and beyond, she'd do it on the active cases sitting on her desk rather than her "obsession."

"You did your homework," Duncan said.

No judgment. No knocking her down, accusing her of going off on wild tangents. He simply chose to believe her. She could almost hear Alanis Morissette crooning the lyrics to her hit song "Ironic," lamenting things like getting a death row pardon a minute too late. Wouldn't that be something? To finally find someone who not only listened to her, but was willing to take a chance on her being right, but the circle was closed? The seventh data point was already on the map. The killer had taken his last victim, and they were too late to stop him. Could life really be that cruel?

Stupid question.

The Jeep bounced even worse as he turned off the road onto a part of the mountain that flattened into a plateau. Dozens of other vehicles were already there. Several groups of people were heading into the trees, either on foot or doubled up on ATVs.

She held on tight to the handle, wincing when her shoulder hit the door. When the Jeep finally stopped, she eased her death grip and gingerly lowered her arm.

They were high up on the same mountain she'd been on this morning. It seemed so remote, isolated, until she noticed the cell tower on the right side of the field. Ahead of them, McAlister already had his tailgate down and was hooking up a ramp to unload the ATVs. Special Agent Lee and Ranger Grady were standing beside McAlister. They must have heard about the missing woman and headed straight to the site without stopping at the trailer.

"Wait here." Duncan kept the engine running and hopped out to talk to his coworkers. A few moments later, he got back into the Jeep. He set a small white bag on the seat between them and then leaned across her to open the glove box. The utility belt she'd seen him wearing this morning—had that really been only this morning?—was in the compartment. He pulled it out.

"Is your cell phone charged?" he asked.

"Yes. Why?"

He motioned toward the passenger window. "There's the cell tower I mentioned earlier. If you need to make a call, you'll be able to get through. Add my cell phone number to your favorites." He rattled off the number while she keyed it in.

"Stay in the Jeep with the heater on. There's plenty of fuel, so that shouldn't be a problem. Plus…" He tapped the bag between them. "There's a sub, chips and a bottle of water in there that the boss got you for lunch. There are more bottles of water in the back and more snacks if you're still hungry. There's even a blanket behind the seat if you're not warm enough. I keep a go-bag in my Jeep at all times, with all the essentials, in case I end up stranded in a snowbank."

"And your orange backpack."

He smiled. "And my orange backpack, yes. That's a slimmed down version of my go-bag. Something all of us get in the habit of taking if we think there's any possibility that we might be out on the trails for more than an hour or so."

"Why are you offering me a sub and a blanket? I thought I was going with you."

He shook his head. "No way. You're suspended and facing potential criminal charges. I can't have you at a crime scene. But no one's at the trailer right now, either. So for the moment, you're stuck here. I'm sorry about that. But I need you to wait here. Plus, there's something else to consider." He pulled his phone out and scrolled through the text messages. "Lee texted me this when I was talking to him a few minutes ago." He tapped the screen and turned it around. "This is the missing woman."

Remi pressed her hand to her throat. The resemblance was uncanny. "She looks like…me."

"Exactly." He shoved the phone back into his pocket. "Her family's up there with the search and rescue team. I don't want them seeing you and getting hopeful, even for a few seconds, before their brains catch up to their emotions and they clearly see the height difference. Sheryl Foster is half a foot taller than you. Then again, most people probably are."

His smile was a ghost of his former smiles, and she realized he was trying to lighten things up, to make her feel better. He really was a good man.

"I understand," she said. "I'll wait here."

"Thanks." He tightened his hand around the utility belt. "I'm going to assess the scene, but I should be back within the hour. I won't be part of the search and rescue team. We've got people far better trained than me for that. My boss will work with SAR on that end. My job is to coordinate the investigation, get the other investigators already on the scene to conduct the necessary interviews, get the lines of communication set up between the crime scene techs and—"

"Wait, crime scene techs? I thought she was just missing at this point." As if *just missing* wasn't bad enough. "Is there reason to believe something bad already happened?"

"The techs will help us examine her last known location. It's the base of operations, where the search begins. They'll look for evidence to help the SAR team. Once I make sure everything's in place and everyone knows their respective duties, I'll drive us back to the trailer and organize an investigative team on that end. Like I said, I won't be gone long. We've got all hands on deck for this, lots of investigators and rangers being called in. We do this a dozen times a year, like clockwork, every time someone gets lost. We all know the routine. Ninety-nine times out of a hundred, we find missing people in a handful of hours and bring them back home, safe and sound."

Again, he smiled. Again, she wasn't buying it. He was just as worried as she was. But she played along and smiled back.

He left her in the Jeep and hurried toward McAlister, who was waving impatiently for him to hurry up. Lee and Grady must have driven off on one of the ATVs that McAlister had unloaded, because they were nowhere to be seen and one of the ATVs was gone. As soon as Duncan hopped on behind McAlister, the ATV took off across the field, then disappeared into the forest.

Remi leaned forward and peered up at the ominous storm clouds gathering overhead as Duncan's parting words ran through her mind.

Ninety-nine times out of a hundred, we find missing people in a handful of hours and bring them back home, safe and sound.

She didn't have to ask him what happened in that hundredth case. She already knew.

DUNCAN STOOD ON the ridge, a flurry of activity happening behind him as crime scene techs hurried to make casts of footprints before the storm could destroy the evidence. But it was what Duncan had just found that had chills going up his spine.

He knelt beside the outline of two shoes. They were small, he'd guess a woman's size seven boot, with a distinctive pattern on the sole—the same pattern he'd noticed on the bottom of Remi's boots when he'd left her handcuffed on the ground so he could tend Vale's injuries. She'd stood here, looking out through the gap, before Vale and he had come upon her from different directions.

And so had someone else.

Just a few feet behind her, off to the left behind some bushes, were the impressions of another pair of boots, a man's boots. They were about the same size as Duncan's, which told him the man who'd made them was probably over six feet tall. They were pointed toward the ridge, the toe of one print mashed heavily into the dirt, as if he'd squatted down, the way someone would do if he was trying to hide.

If a man had come up here wanting to enjoy the view, he wouldn't duck down behind these bushes and view the gap through the branches. He'd walk out in the open and stand on the ridge, like Remi had done.

The footprints had then turned in a semicircle, as if he'd been here when Remi walked down from the ridge, and watched her. Which meant he was likely here during the shooting. He'd hidden in these bushes and seen the whole thing. Which also meant something else.

Remi was likely right when she'd said someone was echoing her footsteps, sneaking up on her in the woods.

But it wasn't Vale, and it wasn't Duncan. There'd been another man out here shortly after dawn.

And he'd been hunting Remi Jordan.

Duncan straightened and motioned to one of the techs who was processing other footprints down by the trail where Sheryl Foster had disappeared.

"Sir?" the tech asked.

Duncan pointed at the prints by the bush. "Cast these, too, when you get a chance. And send a picture to the SAR team so they can be on the lookout for those prints."

The tech nodded and took out his camera to snap some pictures.

Careful to keep to the side so he didn't step on any evidence, Duncan followed the prints down the slope. They ended a few feet from the AT, behind an other group of bushes. And on the other side, within reaching distance, was a set of yellow evidence tags.

They marked the last known footprints made by the missing woman.

Chapter Eight

Long after the sun had set, Remi leaned against the back wall of the National Park Service trailer, desperate for just one moment where she wasn't being pushed or shoved or in danger of being trampled.

The chaos of ringing phones, fingers tapping on computer keyboards and people yelling to each other gave the appearance of progress, that something was being done that would eventually result in them finding the missing woman and returning her to her family.

But Remi knew appearances could be deceiving.

The same type of activity had consumed the campsite ten years ago after the sun had come up and Remi woke to an empty tent. She'd immediately told her father about Becca going to meet a boy the night before. The rangers were there within minutes. Eight hours had passed from the last time she'd seen her sister to when the search parties headed out to look for her. No trace of Becca was ever found. Only *two* hours had passed from the time Foster went missing and SAR began their search. Yet no sign had been found of the missing mother of two.

"We're leaving."

She turned, surprised to see Duncan beside her, wearing his jacket and gloves. Her coat was clutched in his right hand. In his left was a thick brown satchel stuffed so full of papers and folders that he'd never get it closed. He held her jacket out.

She hesitated, then carefully eased her right hand out of the sling to put her jacket on. He helped her, making the process much less painful than when she'd put it on by herself in the Jeep, while waiting for him to return from the crime scene.

A few moments later, they were heading down the mountain with the Jeep's heater on full blast and the headlights reflecting off the light blanket of snow covering the road.

"Did we leave because of the storm? It doesn't seem nearly as bad as I thought it would be."

He slowed for one of the many dangerous curves on this steep, narrow stretch of road. Snow flurries swam in the headlights like swarms of moths under a lamppost. "The storm is only going to get worse. The winds in the mountains can whip up to hurricane strength at the higher altitudes. Sleet and snow make the going slippery. Visibility will approach zero in a few hours up there." His voice was tight, clipped.

Remi's heart sank. "They've called off the search, haven't they?"

"SAR has taken shelter inside a cave to wait out the worst of the storm. My boss is telling everyone at the trailer to bug out. That trailer is a satellite office, not typically used as a command post for an investigation this big. It made sense to be there today since it's so close to Foster's last known location. But the base of operations will likely switch to one of the larger, permanent structures at a lower elevation, probably the offices in the Sugarlands Visitor Center."

"But not tonight?"

"Not tonight. There will still be people working the case around the clock. But they'll work from home until this storm blows over."

Remi could well imagine the grief and despair, maybe even anger, when the Foster family was informed that the search was being suspended. Her family had been lucky. The search had gone on for a full week before being called off. But even then, her father had been devastated and furious. He'd yelled and begged the park service to keep looking. In the end, he'd gone home a broken man. The day he'd died, he'd been clutching a picture of Becca to his chest, tears rolling down his cheeks. It broke Remi's heart every time she thought about it.

"How long is the storm supposed to last?"

"Two to three days."

She inhaled sharply. "Two to three days? But… Sheryl Foster—"

"Has a backpack of supplies. This isn't her first time camping up here. Hopefully, she'll hunker down in a cave, or the hollow of a dead tree, and keep warm. SAR will be out looking for her as soon as possible."

She wanted to argue, to yell at him and everyone

else that they needed to get back out there and find her. But he was right. They'd be risking more lives if they did.

A few minutes later, at the base of the mountain, he pulled into a parking lot that was empty except for one lone, dark blue car. Hers. But it wasn't blue anymore. It was pristine white, blanketed with snow. He pulled up beside it.

"Even if you had full use of both of your arms, I wouldn't let you drive in these conditions," he said. "There's too much ice and snow and you don't have a four-wheel drive. I'll take you to get your car when the weather clears up. But I figured you might need your purse. You mentioned it was in the trunk." He held out his hand. "Give me the keys and I'll get it for you."

As she handed him her keys, she asked, "Then you're taking me to my motel?"

"Where else would I take you?"

"Technically, I'm still under arrest. I was worried I might be spending the night in the Gatlinburg jail."

"Yeah, well. I'm a big softy. Plus, by leaving your car here, you'll be stranded. There won't be any taxis or Ubers out in this weather. I think I'm safe leaving my prisoner at Motel 6 tonight."

"It's not a Motel 6."

"Close enough."

She arched a brow. "Federal agent salary. I couldn't afford the Hilton."

He grinned. "I'm with you on that. But I would have sprung for a Holiday Inn."

He popped the door open, but she stopped him with a hand on his arm. He looked at her in question.

"Thank you, Duncan. You've been kinder to me than I deserve. I really appreciate it."

He glanced down at her hand. His Adam's apple bobbed in his throat, and for once, he seemed to be at a loss for words. Finally, he nodded and got out.

A few minutes later, with her purse sitting between them, they were back on the road heading toward Gatlinburg.

"I feel bad that you're going out of your way to take me home," she said. "I hope you don't get stuck out in the storm."

"This Jeep's like a mountain goat. And I've got chains for the tires if I need them. Besides, I don't live all that far from your motel. My cabin's in the foothills a few miles from there. Thanks for the concern, though. It's nice to have someone worry about me besides my mom."

She groaned. "Mom? You're comparing me to your mom?"

"Trust me." His voice sounded husky. "That's definitely not how I think of you."

Her mouth went dry. She should have come back with a sassy reply. But intelligent thought seemed to have deserted her.

"Have you lived in Gatlinburg very long?" Good grief, she was making small talk as if they were on a blind date.

"Been here my whole life. I grew up in a cabin at

the top of one of these mountains. My parents still live there. My brothers and I—"

"How many did you say you had?"

"There are four of us."

"Four boys? Your poor mom."

He grinned. "She'd love you for commiserating with her like that. She blames us for every gray hair on her head." His smile faded. "My brothers Adam and Colin still live in the area, while my youngest sibling, Ian, lives…" He shrugged. "Only God knows where. He's about due to pop in again. This is the longest he's gone without any word."

"I hope he's okay."

"Ian's more than capable of taking care of himself. He's definitely not nice or sweet like your sister, Becca. He's the black sheep of the family, the rebel who has caused more than his share of tears and angst." He shrugged. "In spite of all that, he's family and we love him. I'm sure he'll be home soon."

Unlike her sister, who would *never* come home.

He grimaced and glanced at her, regret heavy in his expression, obviously wishing he could take back his words.

She rushed to cut off the apology that she knew was coming. "What makes you think my sister was nice or sweet?"

His eyes widened. "I just…assumed. You're identical twins and you're, ah, well…"

She took mercy on him and gave him a reassuring smile. "*Nice* and *sweet* are two words my sister would never apply to me. And I assure you, that's the last way that anyone would describe Becca. She was never the sugar and spice and everything nice sort of girl. She was more the snakes and snails and puppy dog tails variety, probably a lot closer to your rebel brother. She was impulsive, argumentative and a completely disruptive member of our household. My dad used to say that if he was the drinking type, she'd have made him an alcoholic."

"I can tell by your voice that you loved every hair-pulling, aggravating thing about her."

"I did. I do. I miss her every day."

She shoved back the strands of hair that kept escaping the ponytail she'd fashioned while at the trailer. But her hair wouldn't stay put. She gave up and pulled the holder out, letting her hair fall past her shoulders.

She caught him glancing at her, his throat working as he looked at the long strands. Heat seemed to radiate between them, thickening the air.

They rode in silence as they entered town. But as he turned down the main street, he said, "Seems odd to me that a group of kids from Colorado would come all the way to Tennessee for their senior trip. Especially since you left one mountain range for another."

She shrugged. "It was a compromise. A lot of us wanted to stay in the mountains near home for the trip. Others, like me, wanted to go somewhere we'd never been."

He seemed to consider that, then nodded. "Makes sense when you put it that way." His smile faded. "Earlier you mentioned two potential suspects in your sister's disappearance. Weber and Hendricks? What-ever came of that?"

"Not much. Becca left our tent willingly, to meet a guy. But she didn't say who he was. Since she didn't have a boyfriend at the time, it could have been any of the guys at our camp. It was a high school senior class trip. There were a couple dozen senior guys, easily. And we weren't the only campers. There were several other tents a ways off from ours, other men. But the two guys you mentioned were in our class, and seemed the most likely to me to have been involved."

She clasped her left hand into a fist on the seat be-side her. "Garrett Weber was the most popular and devastatingly cute guy in class. Becca had a terrible crush on him. Billy Hendricks was just as *un*popu-lar as Garrett was popular. He had a crush on Becca. And, to be honest, she played on his feelings, using him as a tagalong if she didn't have anyone else to go with. But it never went as far as he wanted it to go. She was never serious about him."

"What about Garrett? Was he serious about her?"

"Not that I know of. He had a girlfriend at the time. I can't imagine him or Becca ignoring that and run-ning off to meet each other. But she had it for him bad. If he'd shown any real interest, she'd have had a hard time resisting. Between the two, Garrett seems like the one she'd run off to see. But Billy is the one I could picture holding a grudge and wanting to harm her. And yet Billy had an alibi. Garrett didn't. Not one he could prove, anyway. He was in his tent, alone."

"But the police didn't think he did it?"

"Not really. There just wasn't anything in his background to suggest violent tendencies. No motive. And no physical evidence to support that he might have left his tent—no grass or mud on his shoes from trouncing around in the wilderness, no wet or dirty clothes. The whole investigation stalled pretty fast." She shook her head. "It's been hard, really hard. Which is why I want to do everything that I can to help another family avoid missing their loved one the same way."

When he pulled the Jeep up to her motel and parked in front of her door, neither of them moved. She wasn't sure what he was thinking. But a melancholy had fallen over her. She felt like she was about to say goodbye to a good friend, even though they barely knew each other. And she didn't know what to expect in the coming days, whether she'd end up in jail or free, whether she'd end up without a job or helping with the investigation. The only thing she was sure of was that she didn't want to be alone with her memories of Becca and fears for the missing woman. But she didn't know how to tell him that, or even what she'd be asking if she did.

"I guess I'd better go." She reached for her purse.

His hand was suddenly on her shoulder. "Wait."

The seriousness in his tone had her searching his gaze. "Is something wrong? I mean, something *else*?"

"I've been debating this since I left the office. But you deserve the chance to look it over, even though I don't think it will help."

"Look what over?"

He rummaged through the satchel of papers on the floor that he'd brought with him when they left the trailer. He pulled out a manila folder that was several inches thick, and set it on top of her purse.

The folder had darkened with age. It was curling at the edges. Coffee stains colored one corner.

"What's this?"

"Pops wanted me to give it to you. He's been working in the park since before I was born. He documents everything that goes on in the office in thick manila folders. They aren't official in any way. But a lot of times, he puts copies from the official files in there. And he adds his own personal notes, impressions, things you wouldn't list in a report."

He cleared his throat, looking uncomfortable. "I don't know whether you noticed, but the cell in the office trailer is filled with boxes. Aside from office supplies, the rest of them belong to Pops. He went through them earlier and took out that folder. It's a cold case, the disappearance of Becca Jordan."

Remi stared at the folder beside her. "I've read her file. One of the first things I did when I began working violent crimes for the FBI was to request a copy of it from NPS's national headquarters, the Washington Support Office. WASO's file didn't have any record of a Ranger McAlister as having worked on her case."

"They wouldn't, because he's not a criminal investigator. The law-enforcement variety of rangers are park police and everything that goes with that in a wilderness location—including helping search parties and rescuing people who need help on the trails. Not to mention dealing with fugitives on the run, the rare hostage situation. They pretty much do everything—except the actual investigations."

"That's your job."

"That's my job," he agreed. "Or in major cases, like today, we called in more investigators from the Atlanta regional office and a few park sites closer in to help out. My point is, it's not Pops's responsibility to work cases. But he's old-school, keeps notes on everything, anyway. And he can't stand to see a case go unsolved. There have been many disappearances in the Smokies over the years. Most people are found. But, as you well know, some of those cases go cold. Unless someone calls in a tip or new evidence turns up, there's no reason to look into those cases again. So sometimes Pops, on his own time—"

"Reviews the cold cases, tries to solve them."

"Just like someone else I know." He smiled. "Like I said, he's not a trained investigator. I don't think he's ever solved any crimes. And I don't know that his notes will help—especially since his observations are mostly secondhand. He would have helped with the search, of course. But not the investigation, the interviews. Still, maybe something he wrote will help you gain a new perspective. Doubtful, but maybe. It was important to him that I give you the folder."

She swallowed. "Please thank him for me. That was very thoughtful."

"Don't get your hopes up, okay? The odds of you finding out what happened to her after all these years is slim to none. And the odds of you finding her…"

"Alive?"

He nodded. "The odds are pretty much zero. You know that, right?" His voice was soft, almost tender.

"I work in violent crimes. I know the statistics far better than most."

He helped her out of the car and into her room. Then he hesitated just outside the opening. "There's something else you need to know." His gloved fingers curled around the door frame. "When you said you thought someone was echoing your footsteps, stalking you up on the mountain this morning—or yesterday morning now—you were right. I found footprints that told the story. When you stood on the ridge looking through the gap in the trees, a man was watching you from the bushes, and it wasn't Kurt Vale. If Vale and I hadn't come upon you when we did, he might have abducted or killed you. So if you look at the shooting with those facts in mind, it's a blessing what happened with Vale. It probably saved your life."

Chapter Nine

Duncan balanced the tray of disposable coffee cups and bag of food in one hand as he rapped on Remi's door the next morning. The wind made a moaning sound as it blew around the eaves, the storm still raging, though not as hard as last night.

When no one answered, he knocked again, louder this time. He glanced around the motel parking lot behind him. The main drag through town was just a couple streets over. Remi's motel didn't have a restaurant. Had she headed up the street on her own in search of breakfast? Snow covered everything as far as the eye could see. Even though it wasn't snowing right now, it would be again in the coming hours. He couldn't imagine her wanting to venture out in weather like this with a hurt arm. One wrong step and she could lose her balance and wrench her shoulder.

The sound of the lock being clicked had him turning back around, to see a delightfully disheveled special agent blinking at him from the barely open door.

"I'll never forgive you for waking me at the crack

of dawn. What time is it?" Her tone was far from welcoming. In fact, it sounded downright hostile.

He grinned. "Medusa's got nothing on your hair this morning."

She made a halfhearted attempt at finger-combing the yellow bushy halo around her head. If anything, she made it worse. She grumbled beneath her breath and pulled the door open the rest of the way.

He promptly forgot how to breathe.

She was wearing thin gray sweatpants and a gray Colorado Buffaloes sweatshirt. The sling wasn't over her shoulder yet, so she was clasping her hurt arm against her belly. What she probably didn't realize was that it pulled her shirt tight against her, revealing the sumptuous curves of her breasts. She wasn't wearing a bra. And she was cold.

He swallowed, twice. With Herculean effort, he forced his gaze up to eye level. Another swallow, and he rasped, "I come bearing gifts." He coughed to clear his throat, and held up the drink holder and food bag. Good grief, she was beautiful like this. All soft and sleepy and grumpy.

She shivered as if just noticing how cold it was outside. Then she grabbed one of the cups of coffee with her good hand, held it to her nose and inhaled deeply. "You're forgiven." She headed toward a door on the far end of the room. "I need five minutes."

He had a brief glimpse of white subway tiles before the door closed behind her.

He blew out a ragged breath and stepped inside. From the first moment he'd looked into Remi's soft brown eyes and seen the delicate curve of her face, there'd been no question that she was beautiful. It was one of those things he'd ticked off on a laundry list of attributes, as he would when observing any suspect— Caucasian, approximately five feet two inches tall, golden-brown eyes, long straight blond hair, mid to late twenties, attractive. It was enough for a description if he had to put out an alert to be on the lookout for her. But now he knew the rest of her matched the beauty of her face.

Those thin sweats had outlined every mouthwatering curve.

He'd half convinced himself last night, after getting home, that the sizzling attraction he'd started feeling toward her ever since they'd declared their friendship was a product of his natural empathy for the situation that she was in. He couldn't help but want to help in any way he could. But he'd expected that after a good night's sleep, the next time they were together he'd be able to think of her as just a peer, a fellow law-enforcement officer. And he'd be able to get back to the business of investigating Vale's shooting, while his team focused on the Foster disappearance. But as soon as she'd opened that door, he was lost. He really had it bad for Remi Jordan.

Conflict of interest much?

He shook his head and looked around for somewhere to set the food. The room was clean, and surprisingly modern, with a wood-look porcelain tile floor that was so popular these days. Obviously, the motel had gone through some recent renovations. But the reno hadn't done anything about its dimensions. It was just big enough for a queen-size bed, a dresser across from it, and a small round table by the lone window, with two wooden chairs. Since the table was covered in papers, and the dresser was covered with even more, he set the bag on one of the chairs and took the other chair for himself.

He idly sipped from his coffee as he scanned the pages on the table. He'd assumed they would be from the cold case folder he'd given her last night. But then he saw a picture of a constellation, and realized he was looking at her research. Seven white dots that represented stars were connected by lines. To him, it didn't look like a horse at all, let alone one with a horn in the middle of its forehead. He supposed she was right that he didn't have a good enough imagination. But it was the words written by each dot that held his interest.

The rear hoof was labeled Dry Tortugas National Park, Florida, Melanie Shepherd. What he supposed was the rear end of the horse was labeled Hot Springs National Park, Arkansas, Amanda Powell. In neat succession, every single data point had a location and name associated with it, along with a date.

Congaree National Park, South Carolina, Jacqueline Stuart.

Mammoth Cave National Park, Kentucky, Mindy Brooks.

Cuyahoga Valley National Park, Ohio, Rose Walling.

Shenandoah National Park, Virginia, Allison Downs.

And then, written in fresh ink, the newest entry:

Great Smoky Mountains National Park, Tennessee, Sheryl Foster.

"Thanks for the coffee."

He glanced up to see her walking toward him, holding the cup in her left hand. She was still wearing those distracting clingy sweats, but she'd most definitely put on a bra. And she was wearing the sling again. Plus she'd brushed out her halo of blond hair. It was slightly damp, as if she'd wet it down. But it wasn't straight like yesterday. It rippled in waves, some of it forming curls that bounced on her shoulders.

He longed to plunge his hands into her hair and see if the curls were as soft as they looked. It took a good deal of control to try to keep his expression clear so that his completely inappropriate fascination with her didn't show. He really needed to get a grip.

"Curly," he said, stating the obvious.

"Natural curl, a total pain. It takes me a good hour to flat-iron it straight to head out on the trail."

"To offer yourself as bait." He still couldn't believe she'd put herself at risk that way.

She shrugged, then winced and set her coffee on top of a stack of papers so she could rub her hurt shoulder. She looked around, then grabbed a bottle of ibuprofen off the table by the bed.

He leaned over and took it, opened the cap, then handed it back to her. "Why not just perm it straight if your plan was to walk the AT all February until you caught the killer's attention?"

After drinking down three pills, she lowered her

cup. "I considered it. But having already bleached it blond, if I permed it my hair would probably all fall out. Not an attractive look for me."

As much as he loved her hair, he didn't think it would make her any less attractive if she was bald. She was sexy, period. Not just because of her curvy figure, either. She was smart, dedicated and had a wicked sense of humor.

And...he really needed to get back to business and stop thinking about her that way.

He motioned toward the tabletop with its pile of pictures and papers. "How long did you say you'd been accumulating this research?"

"Six months, give or take."

"And before that? Another case of disappearances?"

She nodded.

"What color did you dye your hair for that one?"

"Red."

He swore. "Do you realize how lucky you are that you haven't been killed already?"

She grabbed the bag off the chair and sat down. "Do I smell bacon?"

"You're trying to distract me."

"Yes, I am. Do I smell bacon?"

He reluctantly smiled and let the subject drop. "Bacon, egg and cheese croissants. They're both for you. I ate mine on the way here. They should still be warm. I made them right before I drove down."

Her eyes widened and she peeked inside the bag. "These are homemade?"

He chuckled at the surprise on her face. "*Home-made* is too strong a word. I already had the crois-sants from a local bakery. I just threw some eggs and bacon in grease, slapped some cheese on top and voilà. Breakfast sandwiches. The coffee's from my K-Cup machine. I just tossed it into a couple of dis-posable cups." He took a sip of his coffee and pulled another sheet of paper toward him.

"Oh, my gosh." Her words came out muffled around a bite of sandwich. She set the sandwich down and put her hand in front of her mouth. "Heavenly."

He grinned. "If you like my thrown-together breakfast sandwiches that much, you'd die for my mac-n-cheese. Straight out of the box, powdered cheese. Mmm, mmm, good."

"Amateur. My frozen pancakes top your boxed mac-n-cheese any day." She took another bite of sand-wich.

"You might win that one. I make great pancakes, from scratch."

She blinked. "From scratch? Now you're being cruel."

"Be really nice to me and I might make you some one day." He thumped his finger on the paper in front of him. "You've done a *lot* of research on these miss-ing women. Did your boss let you do any of it on the clock or did you have to do all of this on your own, in addition to your normal caseload?"

She took a quick sip of coffee to wash down her food, then wiped her mouth with a napkin. "All on my own time. My boss doesn't like me doing any of this."

"You interviewed the families?"

"No. That was where I drew the line. This is my project on the side, with no official backing. I couldn't bear to get anyone's hopes up by introducing myself as FBI years after the initial disappearances. The families would have thought I had new leads, that maybe they'd finally get the answers they've hungered for. I didn't want to give anyone false hope."

"That's very insightful of you, and kind. I honestly don't think I would have thought of it in those terms. But I can see that you're right."

Her mouth tightened. "I have the *bonus* of knowing what it's like to be on both sides."

"Then these interviews are from the *original* investigations?"

"That's right. I visited each park, spoke to the detectives who worked each disappearance, sweet-talked copies of their files from them. They were surprisingly forthcoming. I didn't run into one single person who was worried about a Fed butting her nose into their business without being invited. Then again, I guess you could say my status as the family member of a missing woman gave me added credibility. I admit I played the empathy card to get what I wanted." She waved toward the hundreds of pages spread out in front of them. "Not that it did me much good. I haven't come up with one viable suspect."

She took another bite of her croissant while he scanned page after page of interviews, timelines, victim descriptions, witness statements—not that anyone had really witnessed much of anything. Mostly it was people talking about when they saw the person in the days leading up to her disappearance.

When she'd finished her sandwich, she rolled the bag closed with the second croissant still inside and set it on the floor. "What about your team? Have you spoken to them this morning? Did they piece together anything new?"

"Hard to say. Everything we're doing is just background, time lines, things that will eventually help us prove a case in court, if it comes to that. But nothing so far has generated a true lead that will help us find her. Our investigators canvassed miles of the AT yesterday, talked to everyone they came across before we were forced to pull out. My team checked the logbooks in the shelters—"

"Logbooks?"

"I forgot you're a newbie at trail life."

"Newbie might be stretching my knowledge level."

"There are shelters throughout the Appalachian Trail, like the one you stayed at the night before the shooting." He paused. "Why did you stay overnight that particular evening?"

"Stupidity. Wasn't paying enough attention and got surprised when the sun started going down. I belatedly realized I was way too far from my car to make it back before dark. I knew I'd get lost and I didn't want to die of hypothermia. I'd studied the maps enough to know where the nearest shelter was, and headed there."

"I don't remember you having a backpack," he said. "And I don't remember the complainant who saw your gun describing you as having any supplies with you."

"Yes, well. I wanted to have my hands and arms completely free and be ready to react. You were going to tell me about logbooks, I think?"

Her eyes pleaded with him to let the subject of her unpreparedness drop. He was still in shock, and amazed that she hadn't died of exposure without the right supplies. But she obviously felt embarrassed over the whole thing and he didn't see the point in making her feel worse.

He cleared his throat. "Logbooks. Okay. Many of the shelters have them. It can be anything from a spiral notebook to a leather-bound journal. It's like an old-fashioned guest register at a bed-and-breakfast. People leave their names—usually trail names rather than their legal names—along with dates and maybe a few sentences or paragraphs about their experiences on the AT. Or advice for others at the shelter, maybe warning them about some kind of hazard on the trail, or letting them know a water source has dried up in a certain area."

"Sounds like something that would definitely help with an investigation. Maybe we should—"

"Already done. Examining the logbooks at nearby shelters was one of the first things we did. We have pictures online in the case file of relevant pages in the logs. It will take a while to track down the different people who wrote in those logs. And, of course, not everyone signs the logbooks. You didn't."

"I was too busy keeping an eye on the other hiker

in the shelter, that Zack Towers guy, and watching the woods around me. I barely slept a wink that night. Didn't even occur to me to explore the shelter for something like what you just described. I didn't see anything like that sitting out anywhere."

"The one at your shelter was stored in a plastic bag to keep it dry, and placed in a wooden box under the sleeping platform."

"Looks like I have a lot to learn about trail life."

"Only if you intend to hike the Appalachian again."

"Whatever it takes."

Her chin was set in a stubborn line. She was willing to do anything, risk anything, to catch the person responsible for the women's disappearances.

"Funny how I hiked several days without anyone else noticing my gun in my pocket," she said. "Just how well do you know this Zack Towers guy? Maybe he's the one I heard following me. Maybe he called you hoping you'd take my gun away, leaving me without a weapon to defend myself."

He laughed, then sobered. "You're serious? You've pegged Sunny as a serial killer?"

"Why not? He looks harmless, but he's a big guy, capable of overpowering most women easily enough."

"Big as in tall, sure. But he's scrawny. The guy doesn't weigh much more than you. He's got hiker's legs, I'll give him that. But I can't see him coming out the winner in a physical confrontation. He'd more likely turn tail and run."

"You said yourself he's a regular, that he comes up here every year about this time."

He held up his hands in surrender. "Maybe you're right. You never know about people. Everyone has their secrets. But let's start with some background, for my benefit. Walk me through more of your research. Give me the short version of what you've compiled."

"The short version is that I really don't have much. I mean, I have a lot of useless details about each of the victims. I can tell you what they were wearing when they disappeared, who was the last known person to have seen them, why they were in each particular park, even what they ate before they disappeared. But other than their physical attributes and the national park angle, and my constellation theory, nothing I have is helpful. None of them had anyone in their lives who would have wanted to harm them. It seems completely random, a stranger abduction, the absolute hardest kind of abduction to solve."

"I haven't seen any lists of who drove in and out of these parks on the days of the disappearances."

"There's only one." She spread the pages out even more, apparently seeing some kind of organization to the clutter that escaped him. "Here it is." She handed him a small stack that was stapled together. "That's from the most recent disappearance. Well, the one before ours here. Allison Downs, Shenandoah National Park. That particular facility has video of everyone coming and going at the park entrance. Since it's digital and only takes up space on a computer hard drive, they have video going back for years. They let me sit in their security office and create my own paper log of all the vehicles and people coming and going in the few days before and after Allison disappeared."

"You compiled this by hand? There have to be hundreds of listings here."

"Three hundred fifty-seven. And yes, I stared at video for a full week while writing all of that information down. It was a lot of work."

"Impressive. You have license plates on a lot of these, descriptions of the occupants."

"It would be impressive if any of it had led me to Allison Downs. But it didn't. And none of the other parks had any records going that far back. Those disappearances had been years before. So I have nothing to compare my list against."

"We keep video indefinitely."

She straightened. "You have video?"

"I do. It's accessible online in the file-sharing area of our investigation wiki. We've started making lists. I've got someone working on it right now, actually. But it's a painstaking task, as you well know." He pulled the Shenandoah list toward him. "But now that we have something to compare it to, maybe—"

"—we'll see the same vehicle at both parks."

He nodded. "If we get lucky, yes. And if the bad guy drove into the park. He could have ridden in on motorcycle, through the woods, and not even come by the cameras. It's a huge park."

Her shoulders slumped with disappointment. "I'm getting nowhere on this. I could use some help, a fresh set of eyes. What are your plans today?"

"Well, originally, I wanted to come check on you,

make sure you had everything you need until the storm blows over—feed you breakfast. Then I was going back up to my cabin to work on the Sheryl Foster investigation." He cleared his throat. "Plus, I need to follow up on the shooting investigation. I want to check on Vale in the hospital, ask him some more questions."

She stiffened at the mention of Vale. "Make sure you ask him where he tossed the gun."

"I will."

She blinked. "You will?"

He nodded. "When it's okay to go back up the mountain, I'll have someone conduct a broader search of the area with a metal detector."

"Thank you."

"You're welcome. Of course, you know whoever took Foster can't be Vale, right? Even if he did have a gun? Vale is in the hospital. He has an airtight alibi."

"Are you sure about that? Maybe he left the hospital against doctor's orders and—"

"I called this morning. At the time of Foster's disappearance he was with a doctor."

"Nothing's ever easy, is it?"

"It can be less difficult if you team up with someone and help each other. Do you want to work together?"

She straightened. "Don't tease me. That would be cruel."

He chuckled. "I need to keep an eye on you anyway, at least until I get with the DA on your case. I can't think of a better way than to take you up to my cabin. I'll let you view the video and whatever lists my team has already put together. You can compare them with your Shenandoah list and see if anything shakes out. Meanwhile, I'll look into some other angles and see if I can't expedite the investigation into Vale's shooting. I'm sure you'd like to get that resolved, one way or the other."

Chapter Ten

Remi sat at the big yellow pine table in the cabin's rustic eat-in kitchen, her laptop in front of her. Duncan had created a temporary login for her and had her hooked to the wiki site his team used for their investigations. And she'd been viewing videos of the park's entrances for hours, freeing up one of his investigators to work on another aspect of the case while she worked on the list. But it was taking forever, and the video was grainy, a lower quality feed than what she'd had in Shenandoah. She was getting a headache from squinting at the freeze frames of the license plates.

When they broke for lunch, she walked around the main room of the cabin, stretching her cramped muscles as she admired the exquisite floor-to-ceiling stacked stone fireplace with a roaring fire popping and snapping inside it. The view out the picture windows was lovely, but everything was white. She imagined it would be breathtaking in the summer, or the fall with the changing leaves stretching up and down the mountaintops far into the distance. Cabins like this, with views like this, didn't come with a federal agent's salary. He either had another source of income, or he was crooked. Even though she hadn't known him long, she had zero doubt that his money came honestly.

Hours later, back at the table poring over reports and videos and lists, she was feeling like a pretzel again. The longer she sat, the more her shoulder ached.

"Looks like you could use some more Vitamin I." Duncan shoved his phone into his pocket and entered the kitchen from the vaulted great room, where he'd gone to make some calls.

"Vitamin I? That's what you call ibuprofen?"

"The drug of choice for all trail hikers. And FBI agents who've been hunched over their computers for most of the day." He grabbed a bottle of pills from a cabinet and set it opened in front of her, along with a bottle of water for her and one for himself. "Just how bad is your shoulder? I'm sure I could make it to the hospital in my Jeep and get you seen by a doctor."

"In this weather?" She motioned toward the large windows flanking the fireplace in the other room. It wasn't snowing at the moment, but trees still swayed in the wind.

"It's not as bad as it was when we drove up here this morning. I think the storm will blow over earlier than predicted."

"Well, my shoulder isn't an emergency. A few Vitamin I's and I'll be as good as new." She swallowed a couple pills.

"Are you this much of a slob at home?" he teased, and started straightening the papers on the table.

She slapped his hand away. "Stop that. I have a system. If you move stuff I won't be able to find anything."

"A system, huh? Prove it. If I want the research on the Hot Springs disappearance, where should I look?"

"Right over here." She tapped a jumble of pages about a foot to his left.

"Lucky guess. Cuyahoga Valley?"

"Here." She tapped another stack.

He arched a brow. "Mammoth Cave National Park."

She pointed to a stack to his right.

He picked up the first page, scanned it, then set it back down. "Okay. You have a system."

"It's not easy being smarter than everyone else. But I bear my burden the best that I can."

He rolled his eyes. The gesture reminded her so much of Becca that her throat went tight.

"Remi?" He touched her hand. "You okay?"

"I'm fine. Just…thinking." She blinked and stared at her computer. But she couldn't quite bring it into focus. She sighed and sat back. "I can't look at these grainy videos anymore, not right now, anyway. You guys need better cameras."

"That's what happens when a bureaucrat in DC sets the budget."

"You were in the other room on the phone quite a while. Find out anything new?" she asked.

"Actually, I was about to surprise you with some good news."

"They found Sheryl Foster? She's okay?"

He winced. "No. Sorry. Didn't mean to give you false hope. It's still a bit too rough out there for the SAR team to resume their search."

Disappointment was bitter in her throat. "What's the good news then?"

"My district attorney friend, like us, is working from home, waiting out the storm. I spoke to him about your case and he agrees with my recommendations. No charges will be filed against you. As of this moment, you're free to go. Or once I can get you back to your car."

She pressed her hand to her chest, some of the tension and pain in her shoulder seeming to magically ease at his words. "I didn't know how worried and stressed out I was about that until now. It's like a boulder has been lifted off me. But I thought you still needed to go interview Vale in the hospital before your final recommendations."

"I did. Over the phone earlier, in the other room. He didn't have anything new to offer to help with the investigation. But he also said he wasn't interested in pressing charges. That's not his decision, of course. But he added that he wouldn't sue you in civil court. He feels guilty for scaring you. He feels partly to blame and said he couldn't in good conscience try to benefit financially when his own actions contributed to what happened. He thinks of it as an unfortunate accident. Period."

She sat there, stunned at the sudden turn of events. "That's certainly unexpected, especially in today's society, where everyone sues everyone over any little thing."

"You don't sound very happy."

"I am. I guess. I just…" She shook her head, thinking back to that moment on the ridge.

Scuffling sounded behind her.

She turned.

A man in camouflage faced her from twenty feet away.

She told him to freeze.

He pulled a gun out of his pocket.

Or had he?

"Remi?"

"I just… I just keep picturing him pulling that Glock out of his pocket. How could he not be our guy?"

He rested his forearms on the table. "You've taken people's statements many times, right?"

"Of course. Dozens of times."

"Have you ever taken eyewitness statements from two people who saw the same thing, and their statements were polar opposites? But you believed both people were absolutely one hundred percent certain about what they'd seen?"

She started to cross her arms, before remembering her sling. Instead, she fisted her left hand on the table. "Every investigator I know has. But that doesn't change what I saw."

"Doesn't it? You need that cell phone to be a gun."

"So I'm imagining a gun that was never there."

"I think so, yes."

She wanted to shake her head. But he could be right. She knew it was possible. People often convinced themselves they'd seen something, because they wanted so hard to believe it. Was that what she was doing now? Convincing herself she'd seen a gun because the alternative was too hard to accept—that she really had shot an unarmed man?

"Just think about it, Remi. Maybe once some time passes, you'll see it differently."

"Maybe," she grudgingly allowed, hating that he might be right.

"As for your job, you're not out of the woods there. I have no idea what your employer is going to decide about your future career with them."

"The bureau was a means to an end from day one, anyway," she said. "My goal all along was to join the BAU. But after this latest episode, I have no illusions about that. Maybe I'll go into the private sector and become a private investigator. I'd have a lot more freedom to pursue the cases that I'm most interested in."

"If you ever want any PI tips, let me know. My future sister-in-law used to work for one and could teach you a thing or two."

"Future sister-in-law? You have a wedding coming up in the family?"

"We do. Jody Ingram is marrying my oldest brother, Adam. They met during a case last summer. His leg was severely injured in an accident in the mountains. As soon as he's recovered enough, they'll set a date. It'll be the first wedding for us McKenzie brothers. Unless Ian got married without telling us.

Honestly, I wouldn't put it past him." He waved toward the stacks of paper. "You wanted a break from the computer. Let's talk it out, throw around any ideas either of us has. I updated my boss and this morning's shift of investigators about your theory."

She groaned. "Great. Now they'll all think I belong in a straitjacket."

"Does it really matter? Personally, I'm willing to consider anything if it will help us find a missing woman, or keep others from suffering the same fate. As far as your theory, one part is nagging at me. I know there are a lot of blond women out there, because so many dye their hair. But how many have long straight hair? And of those, how many go hiking in the parks? It seems far-fetched that he's always lucky enough to find a victim to match his favorite victim criteria."

"I don't agree. It's not like he's targeting a specific day in February. He has the entire month to look through the park, watch people, wait until the perfect woman comes along. Then he snatches her." She waved toward the computer screen, which was dark now because it had timed out. "Trust me. I've seen plenty of women who fit his profile while looking through the videos both for Shenandoah and the Smokies."

He tilted his head, considering. "How many is plenty?"

"I haven't really been counting. But just in viewing the past week from your park, I'd guess that I've seen five or six. Extrapolate that to an entire month and he has twenty to twenty-four potential victims to choose from. The problem now is that, if he took Foster, his pattern is complete. There's no reason for him to stick around. We'll probably never catch him."

"I'm not ready to concede defeat just yet. Let's follow this through. What do we know, or think we know? He has a type, he waits days, weeks, until someone of that type comes along, then he abducts her. What we don't know is what he does after he takes her. If he waits a full year between victims, what's he doing the other three hundred sixty-four days of the year? This guy is cold and calculating, a psychopath. Abducting these women is an addiction for him. He lives for this. Can he really wait an entire year between abductions?"

"Good point. But I looked for other similar abductions. I don't see how I could have missed any, if that's what you're thinking."

"What if he has more than one victim type?"

She stared at him. "I don't… I don't understand. Are you thinking that, say, every six months he abducts someone? Maybe he's working on another constellation with different victim criteria? Like brunettes, or redheads?"

He spread his hands out to his sides. "Just exploring possibilities. Trying to figure this guy out. One victim a year doesn't seem like enough to me. I'm picturing him like a tiger in a cage, pacing around, getting anxious while he watches the calendar. Most serial killers I've heard of kill more frequently, or in clusters. And they don't always stick to a specific

Dear Reader,

IT'S A FACT: if you answer 4 quick questions, we'll send you 4 FREE REWARDS!

I'm not kidding you. As a leading publisher of women's fiction, we value your opinions… and your time. That's why we are prepared to **reward** you handsomely for completing our mini-survey. In fact, we have 4 Free Rewards for you, including 2 free books and 2 free gifts.

As you may have guessed, that's why our mini-survey is called **"4 for 4".** Answer 4 questions and get 4 Free Rewards. It's that simple!

Thank you for participating in our survey,

Pam Powers

To get your 4 FREE REWARDS:
Complete the survey below and return the insert today to receive 2 FREE BOOKS and 2 FREE GIFTS guaranteed!

"4 for 4" MINI-SURVEY

1 Is reading one of your favorite hobbies?
☐ YES ☐ NO

2 Do you prefer to read instead of watch TV?
☐ YES ☐ NO

3 Do you read newspapers and magazines?
☐ YES ☐ NO

4 Do you enjoy trying new book series with FREE BOOKS?
☐ YES ☐ NO

YES! I have completed the above Mini-Survey. Please send me my 4 FREE REWARDS (worth over $20 retail). I understand that I am under no obligation to buy anything, as explained on the back of this card.

❑ I prefer the regular-print edition
182/382 HDL GNUK

❑ I prefer the larger-print edition
199/399 HDL GNUK

FIRST NAME

LAST NAME

ADDRESS

APT.#

CITY

STATE/PROV.

ZIP/POSTAL CODE

READER SERVICE—Here's how it works:

type. Ted Bundy preferred college-aged women with long brown hair parted in the middle. But he confessed to a biographer that his first kill was a man. And one of the early victims that he's suspected of killing was only eight years old. When the need to kill is driving one of these psychopaths, they strike out at victims of opportunity who may or may not fit their ideal preferences. I just think we should look at other disappearances and see if there are more that we might be able to attribute to this same guy. The more data we have, the more likely we'll find mistakes he's made along the way, mistakes that may help us track him down."

"The BTK killer, Dennis Rader, killed ten people. But he went years between kills, one time as many as eight years," she countered, not quite ready to give up the theory she'd worked on for so long.

"He's more an exception than a rule, though, isn't he?" He was equally unwilling to drop his line of inquiry.

"I guess so," she said grudgingly. "Most of them do kill more often. All right. We can do it your way, take another look. But I'm worried we'll spend all our time off on a wild-goose chase."

"Then let's limit our search, and the amount of time we spend on this."

She nodded, still not convinced. "How about geography? If we search the whole country, we could spend weeks, months, going over missing persons cases."

"Not if we limit them to national parks, the sixty main sites. We can even limit it just to the seven sites you already identified, stick with your original theory, just expand on it. For one thing, let's not restrict the time frame. Maybe you found the key abductions in February that form the constellation. But he reinforces that pattern during another season, maybe during the summer."

She punched a key to wake up her computer, and was about to type a URL, then slumped back against her seat. "I'm on administrative leave. I can't get into any of the national databases I normally access."

"We're both Feds. I've probably got access to many of the sites you use. I've looked into plenty of missing persons cases over the years." He rounded the table and pulled a chair up beside her. After logging on to one of the main missing persons law-enforcement databases, he turned the computer back to her. "You do the honors."

They took turns searching various databases, expanding their criteria to include homicides as well as disappearances in national parks, operating on the theory that if there were more victims from this same man, some of the bodies could have been found. There were a surprising number to dig through when homicides were included. They had to weed through suicides, for one. Sadly, aside from falls and drownings as the leading causes of death in the nation's park system, suicide was right up there. Apparently, people found solace in walking into the wilderness and ending their lives up close and personal with nature.

After a quick break for a dinner of grilled cheese sandwiches and tomato soup, they were back at their own computers, considering each case, taking copious notes. Once they felt they had all the cases that could possibly be relevant, they split them up and began eliminating them one by one.

Finally, Remi sat back, staring at the three cases she couldn't rule out. A sick feeling began to settle in her gut as she checked the locations and dates. She felt Duncan's gaze on her and looked up. From the other side of the table, he peered at her over his laptop.

"Verdict?" he asked.

"I have three that I can't rule out."

"Me, too. Read off what you have."

She swallowed, then read the locations. "Dry Tortugas, Cuyahoga Valley and Mammoth Cave."

His eyes widened. "Hot Springs, Congaree, Shenandoah."

She fisted her left hand on top of the table. "You were right. How could I not have seen this pattern before? He's abducting two women every year in the same locations. First a blonde, then a brunette. Maybe more if we missed something else."

"It's not your fault. It's tunnel vision," he said. "As soon as you found the original pattern, you were naturally blind to a new pattern. And we can use this to find him. Even if he took Foster, he's not finished. He's not going anywhere."

"Do you have the exact dates that each of your three victims went missing? I need the date for each one."

"Give me a second. That's buried in my notes." As he located the data, he read it aloud to her. When he finished the last one, he stared at her intently. "I'm not liking the sound of this."

She finished filling in the matrix she'd created for the six new victims, then nodded. "It's right there in front of us. Every time he abducts a blonde victim, he abducts a brunette—"

"Two days later," they both said at the same time.

"If Foster was his first victim, then he's already out there looking for the next one," she said. "He's going to abduct her tomorrow."

"I'll call my boss, have him officially invite the FBI into the investigation. We'll get the teams working on the evidence from the other cases we've found. There's physical evidence in some of these additional cases, forensic evidence on the three whose bodies were recovered. We'll get him, Remi. We'll get this bastard and lock him up."

"But will we get him in time?"

The anguish in his gaze reflected her own. They had less than twenty-four hours to fit all the pieces together, to try to stop a killer from taking another victim. And what about Sheryl Foster? Were they already too late for her? Was she shivering in the snow somewhere, staving off a sadistic man and wondering if anyone was ever going to come save her?

She glanced past his shoulder to check the weather, and blinked in surprise. "Duncan. The storm."

He turned around in his chair.

The pine trees outside the windows weren't swaying in the wind. Everything was quiet.

"It's over. The blizzard has moved on," he said. "Search and rescue can get out there and find Foster." He shoved his chair back from the table. As he stood, he said, "I'll check in with Lee, get a status on SAR, bring everyone up to speed on what we've discovered." As soon as he pulled his phone out of his pocket, it buzzed. He checked the screen, then answered the call.

"Hey, boss. I was just about to…"

Remi watched his face go pale as he listened to whatever Lee was telling him. He listened for several minutes, saying only the occasional "okay." Finally, he said, "All right. We're at my cabin. We'll head there now."

She watched him slowly round the table to where she was sitting. She pushed herself to standing and looked up into his misery-filled eyes.

"What is it?" she asked. "Did they…did they find Sheryl Foster's body?"

"No." His voice sounded strained. "SAR headed back out over an hour ago. They're still looking for her."

"Then why do you look like someone kicked your dog?" She sucked in a breath. "Did he already abduct the second victim, take her early? Another woman is missing?"

He shook his head. "No one else has been abducted that we know of. But the SAR team did find someone. Remi, they found a skeleton."

Chapter Eleven

Duncan walked beside Remi, holding her left hand to help her keep her balance as they stepped over rocks and crunched across fresh snow behind a SAR team leader. Duncan would have preferred not to bring her out here at all. But his boss had insisted. With her hurt shoulder and her arm in a sling, she wasn't as steady as she needed to be, especially going downhill through the woods on steep grades without a true trail to follow. But he knew there wouldn't have been any point in him trying to stop her once his boss told her about SAR's discovery. So here he was, with Lee and a team of rangers and investigators keeping a respectful distance behind them. He hated that he'd forever be linked in her mind with the second worst day of her life, right up there with the worst day—when her twin sister went missing.

Then again, he hated to think of her going through this without having someone with her who cared about her. And he definitely did, more than he would have thought possible in such a short time. Not that it would matter after this. She'd never be able to look at him again without remembering the scene he was taking her to. And that, as they said, would be all she wrote. She'd go back to Colorado, leaving him and her bad memories behind. In her shoes, he'd probably feel the same way. But it still sucked no matter how he looked at it.

"It's not her. The skeleton isn't Becca," she whispered beside him.

He didn't bother replying. She'd been repeating those two sentences to herself every few minutes since the moment he'd told her about the discovery of human remains. They'd been found about a mile west of the gap where Remi had stood so recently, and yet so very long ago, in terms of everything that had happened since then.

Up ahead, the underbrush and trees gave way to a clearing surrounded by woods on two sides, rocks on the other sides. The crime scene techs had rigged a twenty-by-twenty temporary cover over it, orange waterproof fabric attached to four metal poles driven into the ground. And beneath the orange cover, in the very middle, lay a white sheet.

They stopped a few feet from that sheet. One of the techs squatted down, his gloved hand resting on the corner of the fabric as he waited for Duncan's signal.

"You don't have to do this," Duncan whispered. "We can wait for DNA results and—"

"I want to. I need to know. DNA would take too long."

"They'll have to confirm with DNA, anyway. This is pointless. Lee shouldn't have demanded that you come down here. And you don't have to do anything he tells you to do. Let me take you back up the mountain and wait for the medical examiner to do his job."

She tilted her head back, her gaze finally meeting his. "You're a good man, Duncan. You don't know how much it means to me that you care, that you want to protect me. But I need to do this. I need to know. And I need you to understand. Okay?" She tightened her grip on his hand. "Okay?"

"I'm going to have to turn in my man card after this. I'm supposed to be comforting you, not the other way around."

She smiled. "Your man card is safe. You've been comforting me this whole time."

He pulled her to him, not caring who watched or what they thought, and carefully hugged her, mindful of her hurt shoulder. She rested her cheek against his chest and drew a shaky breath. Then she stepped away and tugged her hand from his.

"Let's get this over with." She straightened her back and turned with him to face the crime scene.

He signaled the tech, who pulled the sheet away, revealing a body bag. Duncan had been surprised to see the sheet when they'd approached, thinking the team was compromising the scene by allowing the cotton fibers to potentially mix in with the skeleton and surrounding dirt. But now he understood. They'd already excavated the site, collected the evidence. The remains were in the zipped bag waiting to be transported up the mountain. All that needed to be done now was to see whether Remi could identify the artifacts with the skeletal remains, provide a tentative identification to speed things along. The crime scene guys were trying to soften the blow, be respectful of Remi's feelings.

The same tech leaned down and, this time without waiting for a signal, unzipped the top of the bag and pulled it down halfway. The corpse was exposed from the middle of its rib cage to the top of its skull— a skull that still had wisps of long, dark, curly brown hair, enough to clearly show the woman had been a brunette.

He heard Remi's sharp intake of breath as she no doubt saw what he saw—the gray concert T-shirt with a picture of country music singer Toby Keith, along with a list of concert dates from a decade earlier— the same shirt listed in the missing posters that were in Becca Jordan's file. A fine gold necklace with a star-shaped medallion hanging on the end was draped around her neck and tangled up in what was left of her hair. The necklace looked just like the one from the case file pictures.

They'd finally found Becca Jordan.

Remi crouched down and leaned toward the skeleton. She started to reach toward it, but the tech stopped her.

"Miss, I'm sorry. We don't want to risk cross contamination. You can't touch her."

"Give me a glove."

"Miss—"

"Give her a glove." Duncan crouched beside

her, lightly gripping the back of her jacket to keep her steady.

The technician grabbed a latex glove from a black bag a short distance away and held it out toward Remi.

Duncan took it. "Let me."

Remi nodded and held out her hand. He rolled it on and tugged it down to cover her left wrist. Then he moved back and held on to her jacket again.

With her hand covered, she drew a deep breath, then reached down and grasped the skeleton's jaw.

The tech gasped in surprise and started forward. But Duncan gave him a warning look so he wouldn't interfere. Lee could yell at him later. As far as he was concerned, this was the risk his boss accepted when he'd insisted that Remi come down here.

She was careful, obviously mindful of not wanting to compromise any evidence. But she gently pushed the jaw down, revealing a set of perfect white teeth that had probably cost Becca's father a fortune in orthodontics.

"All the way, please," Remi said. "The zipper. I need you to unzip it all the way."

"I'm sorry, ma'am, but I don't think—"

"Do it," Duncan ordered.

The tech looked past him and Duncan turned to see what he was looking at. Lee stood about ten feet away with the SAR team. Duncan stared at him, daring him to tell Remi no. But his boss didn't hesitate.

"Go ahead."

Duncan turned back to the tech. "You heard him."

Shaking his head the whole time, the man carefully unzipped the bag all the way. He peeled it back, obviously worried about losing any potential trace evidence that might still be with the remains, even this many years later.

Remi leaned down close to the body again, slightly off balance with her hurt arm, but trusting Duncan to keep her secure. He held on tight to her jacket as she gently turned the right wrist, then moved the skeleton's left femur. She closed her eyes, said a brief prayer that Duncan doubted the others could hear, then held her hand out to Duncan.

"You can take it off now."

He peeled off the latex glove and gave it to the crime scene tech, then helped her stand.

"Are you okay?" He searched her eyes, surprised that there weren't any tears. She was holding up far better than he'd expected under these circumstances.

"I don't know." Her voice held a mixture of sadness and relief. She seemed bewildered, not sure what to do next.

"Come on. Let me get you out of here." He took her hand and led her to his boss.

Lee had a somber look on his face as he awkwardly patted Remi's good shoulder. "I'm sorry for your loss, Miss Jordan. I assure you we'll handle your sister's remains with the utmost respect."

"That's very kind of you, Special Agent Lee." She motioned toward the body bag lying beneath the orange cover. "But that's not my sister."

Chapter Twelve

Remi glanced at the others sitting around the table in the NPS trailer. Since the storm had passed and the recent crime scene was so much closer to the NPS satellite office than to the offices in the Sugarlands Visitor Center, Lee had opened up the trailer again for business. Everyone who was anyone was crammed inside.

Someone had brought in a much larger table for the meeting. It sat in the middle of the trailer, since it wouldn't have fit in the conference room. Remi didn't have a clue how they'd managed to get the thing through the door. Maybe the legs came off. She wasn't sure. Didn't care. What mattered right now was that she once again had the attention of the BAU. And this time, they weren't ignoring her or shooting down her theories. They were actually listening from the other end of the conference call while Special Agent Lee and her embarrassed pseudoboss out of Knoxville sat beside each other surrounded by rangers and NPS investigators, explaining what had happened.

"I'm not following." The voice of Chris Jensen,

the lead BAU guy on the call, sounded through the phone's speaker. "How does she know the remains don't belong to her sister? She said at the beginning of the call that the corpse was wearing her sister's shirt and necklace."

Beside her, Duncan gave Remi an encouraging nod. She leaned toward the phone positioned in the middle of the table. "*She* is sitting right here and can speak for herself. My sister, Becca, was a junk food addict. She had five cavities by the time she was eight years old. She was also stubborn and refused to wear her retainer after my dad paid a fortune for braces. Her teeth had already started going crooked again her sophomore year, which was the source of many heated arguments between her and my parents. The skeleton the SAR team found had perfectly straight teeth. And no fillings."

There was the brief sound of someone murmuring to someone else on the other end of the phone.

"More importantly, Becca was fearless and rebellious, a dangerous combination. When she was fifteen, she took a joyride on a neighbor's dirt bike into the foothills of the Rocky Mountains. She had a horrible wreck, broke her right wrist and her left leg. She had a long metal pin surgically placed in her femur. It was never removed. The skeleton showed no signs of any breaks in the leg or wrist. And no metal pin."

"That metal pin could have fallen out over the past decade. Maybe a wild animal carried it off."

The ME was sitting across from her and motioned to let her know he would answer. "I'm Dr. Hennington, the medical examiner. There were no signs of previous breaks or any marks on the skeleton that would indicate use of medical devices such as pins. I've also reviewed the reports in Miss Rebecca Jordan's file that list her medical history. That skeleton isn't Rebecca Jordan."

"Then how did her shirt and jewelry end up on the skeleton?" Jensen asked.

Duncan took a turn at answering the questions. "This is Special Agent Duncan McKenzie. I believe the man who abducted Sheryl Foster is the same man who abducted Rebecca Jordan ten years ago."

"Hold on," Jensen said. "That's a big leap."

"Not at all. It makes perfect sense," Duncan said. "Footprint evidence proves the same man who abducted Sheryl Foster was stalking Special Agent Jordan. I find it impossible to believe that killer would later stage a corpse with the clothing and jewelry of Special Agent Jordan's missing sister and there not be a link. We've got one killer in the park, gentlemen. And he's taunting Special Agent Jordan, letting her know that he's the one who killed her sister."

"All right," Jensen said.

Remi exchanged a shocked look with Duncan. "All right what?"

"I concede the two cases are likely linked. We'll pull the file on Rebecca Jordan and get a team to re-examine that while we work the current case. Any suspects from the old case you can share off the top of your head?"

Remi swallowed against her tight throat. The BAU

was actually going to look into her sister's case again. She couldn't believe it. "Yes. There were two boys at the camp. One has an alibi, the other didn't. But I think you should take a fresh look at both of them— Billy Hendricks and Garrett Weber. And you might want to look into a section hiker who was out here the other night, Zack Towers. I'd like to know whether you can rule him out in Mrs. Foster's disappearance."

Duncan's mouth tightened. He obviously didn't agree with her assessment about the hiker he knew as Sunny. But he'd said his team would take a fresh look at him. Whether they had or not, having the BAU take a look, too, couldn't hurt.

"We'll get right on it," Jensen said.

The room devolved into noisy conjecture as everyone tried to talk over everyone else. Remi sat back. She'd done her part. She and Duncan had opened the meeting with an explanation of her original theory, along with the modifications Duncan had offered about the additional six cases. Everyone had listened intently to her and Duncan when they'd explained their findings. She was being taken seriously, finally. At least by the rangers and NPS investigators. And it felt good.

Except that other than this phone call, she was precluded from aiding in the investigation.

Her official boss in Colorado had refused to reinstate her. The only reason that he hadn't reprimanded her for "brainstorming" the case with Duncan—her boss's word, not hers—was that with the addition of the six new cases occurring exactly two days after the original six, at the same parks, it was no longer a question of whether her theory was right or not. There was no way to explain all those cases as a coincidence or unrelated events. Still, she wasn't allowed to help.

"Want to get out of here?" Duncan whispered next to her ear.

"More than you could possibly know," she whispered back.

He grasped her elbow, and used his body to shield her as he hustled both of them outside. Once they were in his Jeep again, heading down the now familiar road, she said, "I suppose that now that the DA isn't pressing charges, you're released from babysitting duty. You can drop me off at my car and head back to the outpost. I know you'd rather be there helping with the case."

"Not happening. Everything changed the moment we saw that skeleton with your sister's shirt and necklace. The killer did that to get your attention. He's daring you to go after him. And that's exactly what you're not going to do. It's too dangerous. Lee agrees with me. You and I are going to grab your belongings from your motel room. Then you're staying with me at my cabin. Think of me as your official bodyguard. I'm keeping you out of the park until this killer is caught."

She frowned at him. "I know I've been ridiculously emotional and borderline incompetent since I got here, but I can still—"

"Who said that?"

She blinked. "What?"

"You've been understandably emotional about your sister, and this case, with everything that's happened. And because of your stellar investigative work, we now have a good chance at catching this guy and stopping him. As far as I'm concerned, you deserve a commendation, not condemnation. If it weren't for you, no one would even know that we've got a serial killer stalking our parks. Now that we know, we can save lives and put this guy away. The only incompetents around here are your boss, the BAU guys who refused to listen to you and anyone else dumb enough to doubt your brilliant theories."

She stared at him, stunned by his impassioned defense of her. "Thank you, Duncan. You can't imagine how good it feels to finally have someone who believes in me."

He held his right hand out, palm up.

She hesitated, then put her hand in his.

He squeezed it. "You're very welcome."

When he let her go, her body was humming with pleasure from that one simple touch.

"By the way," he said, "I got something for you while we were organizing that conference call." He unzipped his jacket halfway and reached into an inside pocket. When he pulled out his hand, he was holding a familiar-looking hip holster, with a very familiar SIG Sauer 9 mm pistol inside it.

Her hand shook as she took it from him. "My pistol. I was afraid I'd never get it back."

"It's not loaded. But I've got ammo at my cabin. I noticed it was engraved with your name, figured it was probably special in some way. Even though your jerk boss didn't reinstate you yet, I didn't see any reason to hold on to your personal property. As far as I'm concerned, whatever happened with Vale was an accident. And there's no reason you shouldn't have your gun back."

"This means so much to me. It was a gift from my father, on my eighteenth birthday."

"I think I got socks for my eighteenth birthday. And herpes, from Genevieve Landry."

She laughed. "I know it seems odd for a father to give his daughter a gun. But after losing Becca, he was terrified of something happening to me. He was very ill, cancer. Just like my mom, except a different kind. He knew he wouldn't be around much longer. So he did the only thing he could do."

"He gave you his protection, even beyond the grave. I think that's a wonderful gift."

She smoothed her fingers over the engraving. "I miss him. And Mom. And my sister."

"I miss Genevieve Landry."

She rolled her eyes. "You totally made that up."

"You're right." He grinned. "I didn't get socks for my eighteenth birthday."

She shoved him good-naturedly, then ran her fingers across the pistol once more. A tear dropped onto her hand. She gasped in dismay and set the gun in the console between them so she could wipe her eyes. "Sorry. I swear I'm not a crier. This place, everything that's happened here. You. I just… It's all…"

His hand settled on top of hers again. "It's okay to

cry, Remi. You've been through a lot. You don't always have to be tough, especially not in front of me."

She sniffed and wiped her eyes again.

"I'm not wearing a sling on my shoulder," he said, "in case you haven't noticed. Which means I can easily withstand the pressure of a beautiful woman leaning against me." He waggled his brows and gave her one of those sexy grins that seemed to make the temperature in the Jeep go up ten degrees.

She laughed and scooted as close to him as she could with the console between them. Then she laid her head on his shoulder. It fit perfectly, like he'd been made for her.

"I'd put my arm around you if it weren't for the road conditions. I need both hands on the wheel. You'll have to use that excellent imagination of yours and pretend."

She smiled and closed her eyes. "I'm imagining it right now. You're an excellent hugger."

"The best. Any time you need a hug, I'm your guy."

"You're a good man, Duncan McKenzie. I'm really going to miss you when I go back home."

"And here I thought you'd be glad to get rid of me."

"Not a chance."

At the motel, it didn't take long for her to throw her clothes into a suitcase and check out. The place had been clean, the bed comfortable. But she was more than happy to say goodbye and head up to Duncan's cabin. It would be nice to have someone around for a change. For the first time in years she felt hopeful, like things were coming together.

Regardless of what happened with her job, she'd finally connected the dots for real and had teams of people working on finding justice for over a dozen women. If that was her legacy at the FBI, she'd take it. And gladly move on with a smile to a new job.

She closed her eyes and settled against Duncan's shoulder as he started up the road toward his cabin. It was dark outside now. The inside of the Jeep was toasty warm. And even though he was in no way soft, she loved pillowing her head against him. He was exactly what she needed right now, in so many ways. And she selfishly took what he offered, even if it was just a shoulder to lean on.

Warm. She was so pleasantly, wonderfully warm. And comfortable, so comfy. She snuggled into the pillow and pulled the blanket up higher over her shoulder.

Wait.

Pillow?

Blanket?

She opened her eyes, then gasped and sat straight up. This definitely wasn't Duncan's Jeep. And she hadn't been snuggling against his shoulder, at least, not a moment earlier. She was on a bed, cocooned under the covers. The lights were off in the room, but a door was cracked open to another room and a light was on in it. A bathroom. She could see the shiny glass tiles in the shower, the brown marble vanity. She recognized that bathroom. The first time she'd been in Duncan's cabin he'd given her a tour. She was in his master bedroom.

In his bed.

Her pulse, which was still thumping pretty fast from her surprise at waking up somewhere unknown, sped up even more. Just the thought of being in his bed sent a jolt of longing straight through her. But where was Duncan?

As she glanced around, she saw a note lying on the nightstand next to the bed. The moon was full and lit the room with a soft glow. But it wasn't bright enough for her to read the note. She remembered her phone was in her pocket earlier. Sure enough, it was still there. She pulled it out and used the light to read what Duncan had written.

You pretty much passed out on the way here. I figured you needed the sleep, so I didn't wake you. See you in the morning. D.

He'd left a bottle of ibuprofen on the nightstand, too, along with a bottle of water.

She smiled and set the note down. He was a wonderful man, in so many ways. She glanced at the moon and stars visible through the trees in the large picture window at the far end of the bedroom. It was definitely still nighttime; she just couldn't tell how late. A quick check of her phone told her it was a little after ten. Good grief, she'd slept for hours. But Duncan had been right. She'd needed it. She felt refreshed, relaxed, good for the first time in, well, days.

Even her shoulder wasn't nearly as painful as it had been. Maybe in another week or so it would feel as good as new and she wouldn't have to go through therapy at all.

Therapy. She remembered Duncan had a hot tub on his back deck, with an incredible view of his sloping backyard, the thick woods, and miles and miles of mountaintops. It really was a beautiful place. At night, with the moon and stars out, and twinkling lights of other cabins perched throughout the mountains, she bet it was breathtaking. And that hot tub could probably do wonders for her shoulder.

She glanced at her suitcase sitting on the floor by the dresser. Nothing in there would work as a bathing suit, and she certainly hadn't packed one for a winter trip. Of course, if she'd thought she'd end up in a cabin with a hot tub on the deck, she would have. Then again, who needed a bathing suit if they had their birthday suit.

Would Duncan mind? She didn't see a strip of light under the closed bedroom door. He must be in the other bedroom, asleep. If she was quiet and didn't wake him, no harm done. Mind made up, she headed into the attached bathroom for a quick shower. Then, with a big, fluffy white towel wrapped around her body, she shoved her feet into her house slippers and padded across the carpet to the door in the bedroom that led to the deck, which ran along the entire back of the house.

She'd left her sling on the bed, had taken some pain pills and figured if she could just get into a comfortable position in the tub, she could let the jets and the hot water work their magic. She stepped outside, shivering when the chilly air hit her. She carefully closed the door, trying not to make any sounds that might wake Duncan. Then she turned around and hurried toward the tub, about twenty feet away.

The lid was up and the jets were on. She hesitated. Had Duncan used the tub earlier and forgot to turn it off? Or did people leave them on during the winter to keep the water hot? She had no idea, never having had a hot tub. The only time she'd ever used them were at hotels, by the pool. And those were always on.

She flicked her fingers through the water. It was exquisitely warm. Perfect. She couldn't wait to get in. She dropped her towel, carefully stepped over the side so she wouldn't lose her balance with only one good arm and slowly sank into the water. She moaned in delight. It felt even better than she'd imagined it would. She scooted to the back side of the tub where it was shaped into seats beneath the water, and turned around.

Duncan stood ten feet away, staring at her, eyes wide with surprise. He was barefoot, wearing nothing but a towel slung low on his hips. He had one hand on the sliding glass door, which was half-open, and carried a six-pack of bottled beer in his other hand.

She gasped and ducked lower in the water, crossing her arms over her breasts, wincing at the tug on her right shoulder when she did so. "I'm so sorry," she said. "I didn't realize you were coming out here.

I thought you were asleep and hoped you wouldn't mind."

His mouth quirked in a half smile that did all kinds of crazy things to her belly. "I don't mind at all." His Adam's apple bobbed in his throat as his gaze dipped to her arms. Then he looked out over the mountains as he swallowed again. When he looked at her once more, there was no mistaking the impact seeing her naked, even if only from behind, had had on him. The towel did little to hide his aroused state.

She felt her cheeks flush and forced herself to look up, to meet his gaze, as well.

He winced. "Sorry about that. It's kind of automatic every time I see you. Curse of a lecherous mind, I suppose."

"Every time you see me? Really?"

He let out a shuddering breath and dropped his hand from the door. "Oh. Yeah. Every. Time. Can't honestly say that I'm sorry I stepped out when I did. That's a sight I'll probably treasure until my dying day." He chuckled. "But I'll leave you to it. I imagine that hot water will really help that shoulder feel better. I'll see you in the morning."

"Wait."

He'd started to turn away, but stopped and looked over his shoulder at her, his eyebrows arched as he waited.

Struggling with words, she finally waved toward the six-pack in his hand. "Aren't you going to offer me a beer?"

He looked down as if just remembering he was

carrying something. He smiled ruefully. "You gonna come get it or do you want me to bring it to you?"

She flushed. "Well, I'm certainly not going to come get it. I don't have a bathing suit on."

"Yeah." His voice was husky. "I noticed." Without waiting, he slowly moved forward with the grace of a panther, his eyes never leaving hers. He stopped right beside where she was sitting and squatted down. He pulled a bottle out as he gazed into her eyes, and twisted off the cap. "Here you go." He held it out to her.

If he looked down he'd see everything. But he stared at her eyes, and didn't move, didn't look away. He just waited, as if daring her to move her arms.

Keeping her right arm crossed over her breasts, she reached for the beer. Their hands touched, and a jolt of yearning shot straight through her. He seemed to feel it, too, because his gaze heated and fell to her lips.

"Th-thank you," she whispered, taking the beer.

His gaze rose to hers again. "Anytime." He let go of the bottle, watched her pull it to her lips and take a drink. His Adam's apple bobbed again.

She saw the tension around his mouth, his eyes, and she made a decision right then and there. She dropped her right hand.

He blinked, but kept his gaze glued firmly on her face. She saw a bead of sweat break out on his forehead in spite of the chilly air.

She took another drink of beer, then stretched her left arm out, set the beer on the railing and rested her arm on the edge of the tub. She was open to his gaze, her breasts just inches below the water. And she didn't move to cover them.

"Remi…" His voice was thick, deep. "Is there anything you want to ask me?" The bead of sweat rolled down the side of his face. His nostrils flared, like a stallion scenting a mare.

"Yes, actually." She had to clear her throat to continue. "About your eighteenth birthday—"

"I was kidding about Genevieve Landry. She graduated high school a year before I did and never gave me the time of day." He grinned. "Or anything else."

"Then what are you waiting for?" She scooted over in the hot tub seat to give him room.

He dropped his towel and vaulted over the side. She had an all too brief glimpse of muscled thighs and…everything before he plopped into the water beside her. Squealing and laughing, she turned away from the tidal wave that splashed over her, drenching her.

He was laughing, too, and then he was pulling her onto his lap, settling her thighs over the tops of his, feathering his hands around her waist.

She froze, water frothing just below her breasts. Her hands were on both his shoulders, the pain in her right shoulder barely even registering. Nothing was going to distract her from the amazing feel of a naked Duncan McKenzie beneath her thighs, her bottom, his hard erection pressing against her belly as his suddenly serious dark eyes stared intently into hers from less than a foot away.

There weren't any lights on, but there was enough

moonlight that she could see the outlines of the cords standing out in his neck, the taut muscles of his chest rigid, like the rest of him, as if he was stunned to have her there and was trying to hold back. She decided to make it easy for him. Because she had no intention of holding back now that she finally had him exactly where she wanted him. Well, maybe not exactly, but close enough. For now.

She leaned forward, closer, unable to hide a feminine smile of triumph when his gaze dropped to her breasts. But just as she was about to claim his mouth with hers, he lifted his powerful thighs, angling her up, and then sucked one of her nipples into his hot mouth.

She gasped at the fiery sensations streaking straight to her core and dug her fingers into his shoulders. He didn't seem to notice. If anything, he seemed even more turned on, the thick length of him jerking against her beneath the water as he sucked and stroked and kissed her breast. Then he did the same to her other breast, and she almost climaxed right then. Good grief, he was good at this. So good. But even if he wasn't, she would have enjoyed anything he wanted to do to her, with her, because this was Duncan.

As he kissed and caressed and licked his way across the undersides of her breasts, she knew she was finally where she most wanted to be. The fact that she could never live in the place where her family had been torn apart, and knowing he'd never want to leave because his own family was here, told her this was the only time they'd ever be together. There was no future for them. And that nearly broke her heart. These feelings she had were so new that she probably shouldn't trust them. But they were so strong, stronger than any bond she'd ever felt with anyone else, that she knew they were solid, real, and that it would likely destroy her the day she had to tell him goodbye.

He drew back and lowered her, mindful of her right arm, gently moving it in the water to keep it resting on his shoulder so he wouldn't jar her. He frowned when he framed her face in his hands.

"Regrets already?" he asked. "If you want to stop, I will. Say the word."

The look on his face told her he probably thought he'd die if she made him stop. But just knowing that he would stop had all the good feelings coming back. He was a smart, sexy, considerate, incredible man. She was at least half in love with him, somehow, in such a short time. But there was no denying how she felt. And if this night was all she had, she wasn't going to waste it.

"No regrets." She pressed a soft kiss against his mouth, then whispered in his ear, "I'm on the pill, to regulate my body. But the result is the same. It's safe."

He gently pulled her back. "No Genevieve Landrys in your past, either?"

She laughed. "No Landrys in my past."

He grinned again and his eyes went to half-mast. "This is going to be so good." He gently moved forward, pushing her deeper into the water.

"What are you doing?" She clutched his shoulders as he turned with her and sat her back on the seat.

He carefully placed her right hand on what amounted to an armrest on the molded seat beneath the water.

"Loving you." He winked, then disappeared beneath the water.

His mouth fastened on her and she would have bolted out of the tub if he hadn't been holding her thighs. She shuddered and arched against him, her eyes squeezing shut as he did wicked things with his mouth and tongue. She forced her eyes open, wanting to see him. The sight of him there, just below the surface, kissing her so thoroughly, was the most erotic thing she'd ever seen in her life.

She whimpered and couldn't be still, arching and moving against him. He sucked her, hard, enough to make her swear and rise up off the seat from the sheer pleasure that spiraled through her. Then he burst from the water, dragging in huge gulps of air. Droplets cascaded off his golden chest. His eyes were so dark they were almost black as he once again sucked her nipple into his mouth.

"Duncan," she breathed, then moved her hand beneath the water, searching for him. He shifted his hips and guided her, until the long, thick length of him was in her grip. He shuddered against her and moved his hips again, thrusting through her fingers. She wanted him so much she was trembling, wanted to feel him inside her. She wanted him in her mouth, to kiss him as he'd done her.

"Duncan…" She couldn't say more. Her entire body was drawn like a tight spring, ready to come undone.

He moved his mouth to her neck, his hips still gently thrusting as she ran her hand over and around him, squeezing and stroking him beneath the water. Then he took her earlobe in his mouth and she gasped, her palm automatically tightening around him. He jerked in her grip and then pulled back, positioned himself at her entrance. He looked deep into her eyes and grasped her hips. Then he raised up, his chin at the top of her head as he pushed the tip of himself into her.

She whimpered again and fastened her mouth on his neck. He whispered erotic love words in her ear, then braced his hands on the hot tub on either side of her, still pushing slowly, carefully into her, as if he was worried about hurting her. She didn't want slow and careful. She wanted hard and fast. She wanted all of him. And she wanted it now.

Her shoulder was forgotten. She put both her hands on his shoulders and raised her legs, the movement pulling him in deeper. His whole body shuddered, and then, as if a rope had broken and his restraint was gone, he moved hard and deep into her, filling her, over and over, the water splashing and slapping between them. Tears of pleasure and joy flowed down her face, but she didn't care. This was Duncan, inside her, loving her, and she wanted to treasure every movement, every ounce of heat, every plane and angle of his body as he shared it with her.

She grasped his hips, then gripped his hard, tight

bottom, pulling him to her, pushing her own hips against him. They rode each other hard, each giving and taking, sharing their bodies, their hearts, their souls until the world around them disappeared. Until everything centered on the building pressure between them.

She climaxed first, her body bowing up, her knees coming out of the water as her body milked his. He came moments later, his shaft tightening so hard inside her that she climaxed again before the ripples of her first one had subsided. Then he slowly, ever so slowly, lowered himself back into the water. He collapsed on the bench beside her and pulled her on top of him, his hands going around her waist.

They were both breathing hard, their ragged breaths frosting in the chilly air. But she was anything but cold. As boneless and limp as she felt after their acrobatics, she imagined that she might have slid under the water and drowned if he hadn't draped her body over his and held on to her. But she would have died happy.

She rested her cheek against his chest, his right hand gently gliding up and down her spine, her thighs cradling his. Where he'd been hard and thick against her before, now he was soft and warm, his sated length pressed against her beneath the water. It felt…right, being held in his arms like this, as if he cherished her as they came down to earth together.

Gradually, the world around them seemed to come into focus again. Some kind of night bird made a deep throaty sound from the woods. A soft breeze, nothing like the violent storm of yesterday, rustled the leaves on the trees. The water bubbled and frothed around them.

"I could lie like this forever," she murmured against his chest. "I need a Duncan pillow."

He chuckled and swept her wet hair back from her face. "I'm happy to be your pillow anytime." He moved his left hand up to her right shoulder and gently massaged it. "How's the shoulder?"

She winced and pulled back. "On fire. I was able to ignore it earlier. But all this…" Her face flushed hot again. "All this *activity* has it aching, in spite of the hot water and the ibuprofen I took."

Guilt flashed across his face. "I shouldn't have—"

"Oh, yes you should have. Trust me. The pain is worth it."

He grinned. Then he kissed her, thoroughly, and once again his body began to harden against hers below the water. When he pulled back, she could see desire tightening his features, darkening his eyes.

"You're kidding," she said. "I feel like a limp noodle here. And you're already, ah…"

"You're adorable when you blush," he said. "But we need to get you out of this water before you turn into a prune. And we need to immobilize that shoulder. Let's get you back inside and to bed."

"Only if you're coming to bed with me."

He waggled his brows. "Invitation definitely accepted." He turned her in the water with her good side against him, one hand supporting her thighs, the other around her waist. "I'm going to lift you out. Brace your hurt arm."

"I can get out on my own. You don't have to pick me up."

He started to lift her.

She grabbed her hurt arm and pulled it against her chest as he rose out of the tub like a Titan rising out of the sea. Water cascaded off both of them as he effortlessly stepped over the side with her cradled against him. With no concern for the trail of water they were leaving in their wake, he carried her into his bedroom.

Chapter Thirteen

Remi shoved her plate of pancakes away and sat back in her chair. "Enough. You're like a drug dealer, pushing all this food on me. I won't be able to roll out the door if I eat all of this. I thought you were Irish?"

He blinked, in the process of clearing both their plates from the kitchen table. "I am. Or at least my grandparents are, on both sides of the family. What's that got to do with you not eating enough?"

She rolled her eyes. "From the mounds of bacon, potatoes, eggs and pancakes you've been throwing at me this morning I'd have thought you were Italian. Don't they have traditions of seven-course meals or something like that?"

That sexy grin of his made another appearance, sending her pulse into overdrive. "Throwing food at you, huh? A food fight could get very interesting."

"I'm being serious."

"So am I." He waggled his brows.

She couldn't help it; she laughed. "You're incorrigible. I have a hard time believing you're not the black sheep of the family who caused all the trouble growing up."

"I never said I didn't cause any trouble." He winked and carried the dishes to the sink.

Remi sighed, then cleared her throat in case he'd heard her. The man didn't need any encouragement to distract him once again from work. If he thought she was getting all lovesick over him he'd cart her off to the bedroom, again, and they'd spend another hour wrapped in each other's arms. Not that she didn't want to. Good grief, the man was incredible and she loved being with him. But the time for sleep—and extracurricular activities—was long over. The sun was up. It was a new day. And they had a killer to catch before someone else died.

"You look like you're trying to solve the world's problems."

She pulled over one of the stacks of research folders that they'd moved out of the way for breakfast. "We'll work on the world's issues next. First, we need to see if there's something else we've missed on this case, something that might help Lee and the others find Sheryl Foster and the man who took her."

His heavy sigh was more of his teasing. She knew that. Because he was already reaching for his own set of folders. And she knew that he was just as dedicated to the case as she was, if not more. He was the one who'd practically pushed her out of bed this morning, saying they had a long day ahead of them and needed to get to it. That day included them doing everything they could remotely, from the cabin—since Lee still didn't want her near the park—to try to piece clues together and help in any way they could.

It was close to midday when they both sat like zombies, tired from lack of sleep and frustrated from having come up with no new leads.

"I don't get it," he said, shoving a pile of folders away from him.

"What don't you get?"

He waved his hand as if to encompass all the paperwork on the table. "The logistics. How he's abducting these women and making them disappear so completely, so quickly. How does he escape the net, and then manage to stage a skeleton from a previous kill all under SAR's noses?"

"Maybe he has a car waiting somewhere obscure and has his route mapped out. He grabs the woman, holds her at gunpoint and makes her double-time it to his car. Then he ties her up in his trunk and is miles away before SAR is even looking for her."

"We're talking midwinter. There's lots of snow on the ground. If you're really careful you can mostly stick to rocky soil or step under heavy tree canopies so you don't leave as many prints. But you have to leave some. And how do you get your victim to walk as carefully as you? Seems like we'd have to see more footprints."

She shrugged, then winced and rubbed her shoulder. "Could he drug his victims? Knock them out and carry them?"

"If he went a very short distance, sure. But even someone small like you carried over someone's shoul-

der is going to make hiking through icy rough terrain
a lot more dangerous and strenuous. And his footprints would be heavier. It would be a lot tougher to
hide the path he took." He shook his head. "There
has to be another explanation for how he's getting
his victims out of the immediate area without leaving a trace."

She nodded, remembering the crunch of frozen
ground when Vale had been behind her. "He doesn't
march them out of the area. Then, what? Could he,
I don't know, drug his victim, toss her on his shoulder, then rappel off one of the cliffs and get away?
That could explain the lack of footprints. But I have
no idea if it's even feasible."

Duncan stared at her so long she glanced down
to see if she was having a wardrobe malfunction or
something. Nope. Her T-shirt was in place, the sling
over it with her arm nestled inside.

"You might be onto something," he finally said,
as if he'd been thinking it through. Then he nodded,
"Yes, that could work."

"Rappelling?"

"No. At least, not in Foster's case. Her family
wasn't that far away. Even if the killer had his equip-
ment set up and ready to go, the buckles and har-
nesses are noisy. Suppose he wrapped them in cloth
to mute the sound, the whole process of going over
the side, feeding the rope, pushing off the mountain
with your boots—it's a lot of work and it's not quiet.
He'd be doing it with a body strapped over his shoul-

der or across his back. Again, not easy, and definitely not silent. Her family would have heard him."

"Okay, but you said I was onto something."

"And you might be. What's one of the first rules of training when you're clearing a room?"

"Look everywhere. Side to side, down and up."

"Exactly," he said. "There's another dimension on a big mountain to consider, one we haven't thought about before. We haven't looked down, *inside* the mountain."

"Inside? What do you mean? Like, caves? Caverns?"

"They're all over the Smokies. None up on that part of the trail where Foster's footprints stopped. But what if there are caves beneath it? And some way to get to them quickly and easily?"

She slowly nodded. "I never would have thought of that. But it makes sense."

He pulled his phone out. "I'll call Lee and have him send some searchers out to the last known location of Sheryl Foster and see if they can find a hiding place underneath. They might have to rappel down that cliff themselves to get the lay of the land. From there, maybe they can figure out whatever device or trick our bad guy is using." He punched in his boss's number.

Chapter Fourteen

Shortly after lunch, Lee called back. The look on Duncan's face as he listened to his boss was a mixture of excitement and wariness. Frustrated at not being able to hear what was going on, Remi cupped her ear.

Duncan smiled. "Hang on, Lee. I'm going to put you on speaker so Remi can listen, too." He pressed a button, then set his cell phone in the middle of the table. "Go ahead. You said you found something."

"A trapdoor, up on the ridge, right in the bushes where you saw his footprints. One of the bushes was part of it. There was a foot of dirt on top of the door and the bush was growing on it. After the team hiked down the mountain and came up from below, they saw an opening, a cave below the ridge. So they had someone aboveground looking for a way in while they climbed up. Long story short, the trapdoor is pretty sophisticated. It's heavy and operates on a hydraulic system. Once activated, it pops up about two feet high. Roll something into the opening and slide in after it, and down you go. It's just big enough to hide a body and give him room to, well, do whatever serial killer bastards do when they abduct someone."

Remi clutched her left hand in a fist, her breath coming out in shallow bursts as she waited for the rest. No matter how much she tried not to think of her sister, she couldn't simply pretend that Becca wasn't a part of this. Had she been in that cave? What had the man who'd taken her done to her?

Duncan kept his gaze glued on her as if trying to lend her his own strength.

"We're sending in an electronics expert to examine the door and how it operates. But the prevailing theory is that it can be opened or closed by a cell phone."

"The guy planned this for a long time," Duncan said. "What did you find inside the cave?"

"We found Sheryl Foster. The medical examiner thinks she was dead within the first hour after she disappeared. She was already dead before we started looking for her."

Remi's heart lurched in her chest. She fought back the burn of tears and kept her composure. But she sent up a silent prayer for Sheryl Foster's family.

"There was evidence that another body may have been in the cave at one time," Lee continued.

Remi tensed.

"The ME thinks it was the skeleton we found yesterday, based on a visual of the soil samples from both locations. Obviously lab testing will be required to confirm the theory."

Remi drew a ragged breath.

"We're notifying teams in the other parks to look

for caves and trapdoors in the vicinity of where victims may have been last seen, in case he uses this same MO in those locations."

After the call ended, Remi told Duncan she needed to be alone and went into the bedroom. She sat on the bed, hugging a pillow to her chest as she tried to center herself again. She wanted to find Becca, put her to rest once and for all. And being pulled back and forth these past few days, thinking her sister had been found—twice now—then realizing she hadn't been, had her in emotional turmoil. She wasn't sure how much more of this she could take.

She reached for her cell phone, thinking to pull up some pictures of Becca, to remind herself of the good times they'd had so very long ago, to buoy her spirit. But her phone wasn't plugged in and charging beside the bed. Because, of course, this wasn't her motel room or even her room back home. Duncan had carried her in here last night. It hadn't occurred to her this morning to get her charger out of her luggage or her phone out of her purse and charge it. By now, the battery was likely dead.

Drawing a deep, bracing breath, she straightened and thought about Duncan instead. He was like a rock in a storm. Nothing seemed to faze him. And right now he was in another room in the cabin, working on the case that she should be working on. She could do this. She had to do this, now, before the killer went after someone else, the brunette to finish his two-victim routine. Sitting around feeling sorry for herself and missing her sister wasn't helping anyone. She tossed the pillow aside and went looking for Duncan.

She found him in the family room, with a roaring fire blazing in the fireplace flanked by two enormous picture windows overlooking the mountains. He was pacing back and forth, talking on his cell phone at the other end of the room. There were papers in his hand that he kept referring to as he spoke, but she couldn't make out his words. More papers were spread out on the floor around the couch, and on the coffee table. He was getting just as messy as her.

She sat on the couch and he looked back, smiling as he signaled that he'd be off the phone soon. Once he ended the call, he crossed to the couch, his look of concern turning to surprise as he sat on the coffee table facing her. "You're okay?"

"I'm good. Just needed a few minutes. I'd really hoped to find Mrs. Foster alive."

He grimaced. "Me, too."

She waved toward the papers scattered around. "Bring me up to speed. Let's catch this lowlife."

He leaned toward her and gently cupped her face. "You're an amazing woman, Remi Jordan."

He gave her a quick kiss, then moved back before she could even respond. She longed to follow him, climb onto his lap, curl around him like a cat and never let him go. That shocked her, forcing her to keep her hands off him like nothing else would have. How far gone was she that she could even think about wanting, needing this man, with everything else going on right now? If she wasn't careful, she'd fall in love with him. And that was a dead-end road to nowhere.

"That was Jensen on the phone. He's convinced that Becca was the killer's first victim. That changes everything."

She grew still, stunned. She'd studied profiling and serial killers enough over the years in her quest to join the BAU to understand the significance. "First kills are often someone the killer knows."

"We need to look at the people Becca knew," they both said at the same time.

"Talk to me about your sister. Tell me everything."

"Everything will take too long."

"Focus on the last year, her senior year in high school. You already mentioned Hendricks and Weber, and the BAU is looking into them. Tell me more. Who were her friends. Did she have any enemies. Just say everything you can think of—thoughts, impressions. Don't worry about facts. Do a brain dump about everyone she came into contact with on a regular basis, even if they weren't in her immediate circle of friends. It could be someone who watched her, resented her because she wouldn't date them. No clue is too small." He pulled his computer onto his lap and typed as she spoke.

It was slow going at first, dredging up memories buried for ten years. But she closed her eyes, at Duncan's insistence, and tried to put herself back in high school and remember. Everything. Duncan coached her to think about the smells, the sweaty locker room from gym class, or pizza in the cafeteria, whatever it took to help her get back to that place in her mind. And just like the smell of irises, daffodils, pansies and pink roses in her mother's garden back home always made her feel like her parents were with her once again, those high school smells had her walking the halls in her mind, and seeing her sister's beautiful youthful face.

The words flowed. The memories she'd forgotten were unbottled and came spilling out. She was laughing and crying as she gave him everything she had, until she was spent. Where he'd always been so kind and gentle with her in recent days, Duncan reverted back to his all-business persona, pushing her harder, demanding answers, names, making her dig deeper when she thought she couldn't remember. And it worked. She remembered far more than she ever thought she would. And then, finally, he relented and got her a bottle of water. Then he sat in front of her and began reciting back the highlights he felt were most relevant, and the list of people—all potential suspects—that he'd drawn up.

"That's positively frightening to think there were that many guys in her life who might have wanted to harm her," she said.

"I'm sure most of them would never have wanted to hurt her. But each one of them was significant in some way, or might have had a reason to feel rejected. We have to examine them all. Based on the footprints I found up on the ridge, our guy is probably six feet tall or more. Do you remember any guys that tall at the time of the senior trip? Granted, guys can still grow after high school. But does anyone come to mind from back then to give us someone to focus on?"

"I can only think of a few, maybe five or six."

"Are Hendricks and Weber two of them? Those are the names that you keep bringing up."

"They're the main ones I remember, ones my sister knew. And yes, both were six feet or close to it."

"Earlier you said Hendricks, this Billy guy, had an alibi."

"He was with another girl in the camp that night, Felicia Reynolds."

"Are you sure? Did you ask the girl?"

"Well, no. But the police did. It was in their reports."

"Tell me about Weber. You said he was popular."

"Everyone had a crush on him, including me. But he had a girlfriend. And as far as I know he'd never two-timed anyone before. But even if he would, my sister wouldn't. Becca was all about girl power, a dyed-in-the-wool feminist in the making. She would have never poached another girl's guy." She shook her head. "There's no one else I can think of that she'd have gone off with. But she was super outgoing, and in that guy-crazy phase of life. I suppose it's possible that someone else on the trip caught her eye. I've looked into everyone at the camp over the years and didn't get anywhere. I don't think this is helping."

"Well, I'm new to this case, so bear with me." He grabbed the cold case file that Pops had compiled. After flipping through it halfway, he pulled out a sheet of paper and handed it to her. "That's the list of all the kids on the trip. Even though you've seen a list like that before, take a fresh look. If you were Becca, who might you have gone off to see?"

She sighed and looked at the list. "Got a pen?"

He pulled one of the drawers in the coffee table open and handed her a pen.

She crossed off the ones that she knew her sister didn't like at all. Crossed off two who'd had girlfriends. "That leaves three, including Billy. But I know the police, and the Park Service investigators at the time, looked into all of these. I don't think we're onto anything new."

"Maybe, maybe not." He thumbed through the file. "There aren't any pictures in here. I don't suppose you happened to bring your school yearbook with you."

"Totally slipped my mind. Usually I pack it." She rolled her eyes.

His fingers flew over the keyboard. A moment later he scooted closer beside her with her high school's website on the screen. She was excited at first, but both of them realized quickly this was a dead end. There wasn't an archive section or old yearbooks on the site, just the current school year photos.

Next, he did a web search on Billy's name. But it was a fairly common name and too much came up to be useful. Something she'd learned herself over the years.

"What about one of those ancestry, family tree websites?" he asked. "Maybe someone has a public family tree with him listed and has photos and other facts about him, or the other two, that might help us."

"I never thought of that," she admitted. "Are you a member of one of those sites?"

"Nope. Maybe I don't have to be to perform a search." He pulled up several, and all of them required membership. He pulled out his wallet and used a credit card to join the most popular site. "Remind me to cancel my membership later. This stuff is expensive."

She smiled and together they explored the site, searching all three names. But nothing useful turned up. Billy wasn't on any of the trees they found. And what they found of the others didn't really provide anything pertinent to ruling them in or out as suspects.

"Let's go low tech for a minute." He set the laptop aside. "Tell me about Billy, specifically, since he's the one you first thought of as a suspect. You said she teased him?"

Her face heated. She felt as if she was being disloyal to her sister. But this was important, so she continued. "Becca was a bit…wild. She liked to have fun. Billy was good-looking but kind of a nerd. So when we were in school, she pretty much snubbed him. Everyone knew he liked her. But she didn't give him the time of day. But outside of school, sometimes, well, she led him on, let him take her on dates or to the movies. But it was never anything serious. He just wasn't, well, cool enough for her to be seen with by her friends."

"Ouch. I can see that damaging a young guy's

fragile ego." He held up his hands. "Not that I'm saying your sister was bad for doing that. She was just acting the way teenagers often do. But if Billy is the sociopath type, that could be a potential trigger. I think we need to focus on him to at least try to rule him out." He tapped his knee, looking thoughtful. "We need to look into his alibi. We need to talk to Felicia Reynolds."

Thanks to the FBI, they had Felicia Reynolds, now Felicia Swanson, on the phone in ten minutes. Duncan's face was grim when he ended the call.

"She lied. Billy wasn't with her all night. He was only with her from midnight on. Your sister left your tent around ten."

Remi pressed her hand to her chest. "Why would she lie about that? My sister was missing."

"She didn't believe that Billy was the kind of guy who would hurt anyone. And she liked him. So she didn't think she was hurting anyone by lying. She felt she was doing good, by keeping the investigation focused on people who might have had something to do with Becca's disappearance. She swears even now that she knows Billy would never have hurt Becca."

Remi fisted her hands beside her. "I can't believe she could be that stupid. What's a killer look like, anyway? Ted Bundy was good-looking, wore a suit, went to college. No one would have ever pegged him as a killer, but he was a monster who brutally murdered dozens of women."

"Let's focus here. Billy may not be our guy. Are

there any pictures of the senior trip that you can access on my laptop? I'd like to see this Billy, plus the other guys who were there."

She started to shake her head, then stopped. "Wait. Becca's website. My dad, after Becca disappeared, set up a website trying to spread the word about her disappearance and get people to search for her. I look at it about once a year, when the web-hosting bill comes due. I always think about canceling the service, letting the site go. But then I wonder how my dad would feel, and I pay the bill. Keep the website active another year. There are lots of pictures of her friends, from school, probably from the trip, too. Dad put everything he could think of online and encouraged people to post comments and clues, whatever they thought might help." She told him the URL.

He brought up the site and she pointed out the various people in her and Becca's life from back then. He was paging through several shots taken at school when he stopped and backed up to a previous photo. "Is this you and your sister?"

She leaned in and smiled. "Yep. That was during our junior year. Becca went blond for several months. I'd forgotten about that."

He stared at her. "But you stayed a brunette. Twins—one blonde and one brunette."

Her smiled faded. "One blonde. One brunette." They exchanged a long look.

He turned back to the screen and pointed just past Becca's shoulder. "Who is that?"

She blinked. "That's Billy. And he…he looks… angry."

"Furious is more like it. Do you have any idea why?"

She shook her head. "Knowing Becca, it could be anything. Like I said, she strung him along, but ignored him at school. Let's say he was mad enough to…kill her. Where would the constellation stuff come into play? He wasn't all that smart. He certainly wasn't into astronomy. He was more the remedial science kind of guy who barely managed to pass each year."

"Did he know your sister was into astronomy?"

"Everyone did. But he couldn't have known about the unicorn constellation, unless he was in our bedroom and saw it taped to the wall. And that, I can promise you, never happened. She might have been a tease with Billy. But she would never have brought him home without me knowing, certainly not into the bedroom we shared."

"Was your house a yellow two-story?"

"Yes, but why—"

He clicked the home page tab, then zoomed in on a collage of pictures she'd seen hundreds of times over the years and had gotten so used to that she never really *saw* them anymore. The first one was her family, all four of them standing in the front yard of their home, her mama's beautiful flower garden behind them and the two-story yellow house behind that.

The second was of Becca standing in front of the wall of the bedroom the two of them had shared, with her pride and joy behind her—the picture of the unicorn constellation.

Remi's hand shook as she ran a finger over her sister's outline, then the unicorn behind her. "He knew, about the stars."

Duncan set the laptop aside. "What color was Becca's hair during the senior trip?"

"Brown. Which is one reason why I never connected her disappearance with the missing blonde women. But then, if it is Billy, that kind of makes sense, doesn't it? If he had some sick fantasy, an obsession, with Becca, maybe in his mind he's killing her over and over again. He kills blondes to kill her when she was a blonde, and brunettes for when she was a brunette. Psychopaths don't exactly follow the kind of logic we use. In their minds, that might make sense."

"We need to find Billy Hendricks."

Something bright flashed in Remi's eyes. She blinked and instinctively moved to the side, then gasped at the red dot of light on her left shoulder.

"Get down!" Duncan grabbed her arm and yanked her with him to the floor.

Boom! Glass exploded behind them, raining down onto the hardwood floor like pennies bouncing off a metal roof. Feathers floated through the air like snow.

Duncan twisted against her. He heaved the massive wooden coffee table onto its side and pulled her with him behind it.

She risked a quick glance over her shoulder and saw the bullet hole in the middle of the couch cushion where the feathers must have come from. She looked back the other way, toward the windows, but Duncan and the coffee table blocked her view. The table was solid, thick wood. But could it block a shot from a rifle? She had no idea. They needed to move to a safer location, especially if whoever had fired at them was still out there.

"Duncan, someone's—"

"Shooting at us. I know. They're up high, probably in one of the trees behind the deck."

Boom! Boom! Duncan swore and shoved her against the floor. Feathers floated around them. More glass rained down, tinkling as it landed on the hard surfaces around the room.

"He's at our two o'clock," Duncan said. "And he's got a scope with a laser sight. If I hadn't seen that red dot on your arm, he'd have hit you. We need to get out of here." He looked left and right as if weighing the distances between various pieces of furniture, while keeping both of them out of the line of fire by staying below the top edge of the table he'd upended.

"My gun is in the bedroom," Remi said.

"So is mine." He sounded disgusted with himself. He looked around, then grabbed a handful of glass shards from the floor. He tossed them past the left edge of the coffee table.

Boom! A hard thunk shook the table and little pieces of wood puffed up from the edge.

"That's some hard wood," Remi said. "Remind me to kiss whoever made your table."

He gave her a lopsided grin. "It's mahogany. I'm sure Dad will enjoy that kiss. At least until Mom slaps him."

She laughed and shook her head. "I can't believe you have me laughing when someone is trying to kill us and my shoulder feels like it's been twisted out of its socket all over again."

"Ah, man. Did I do that?" He started to reach for it.

She pushed his hand away. "You saved my life. Don't you dare apologize for wrenching my stupid shoulder."

"I really need to force you to see a doctor now."

"If we survive this, you won't have to force me. Forget Vitamin I. I want the hard stuff."

He snorted and looked around again. "All right. Here's what we're going to do. We need to keep this table between us and the shooter. I'm going to scoot it about a foot to the left. We have to scoot with it. I just need a couple of feet and then I can make a run for the fireplace."

"What do I do?"

"Your job is to stay here and not get shot. I've got a hunting rifle hanging over the mantel and a box of shells underneath it. I'm going to grab that and circle around and take this guy out."

"If you lay some cover fire I can get to the bedroom and grab my gun."

He leaned toward her, forcing her back against the couch. "A pistol doesn't have a chance against a rifle with a scope and laser sight. You stay right here and wait for me. Promise me."

"Oh, good grief, Duncan. I'm an FBI agent, not a helpless civilian. I can get my gun and circle around from the other side. We can flank him and catch him."

Boom! Boom! Boom! Thunk, thunk, thunk. Pieces of sawdust filled the air as the battered coffee table gave up little bits of itself.

He arched a brow at her.

"O…kay. I think I'll just lie right here until you get back."

"Good idea. I'll move the coffee table on three. Draw your legs up."

She drew her legs up.

"One, two, three." He heaved the heavy piece of furniture toward the left, scooting his body behind it as he did.

She scooted along with him, and was glad that when he'd yanked her off the couch he'd managed to pull her down onto her good side. Otherwise, she probably wouldn't have been able to move at all. She wished she could stop and check her shoulder. But every minute they lay here they were putting their lives at risk. The last few shots had sounded like they'd gone a good distance into the thick mahogany. She had no idea whether the next shot might crack the thing in two, leaving them without any cover.

"On three." He counted down. They moved in sync again, then one more time. They'd gone almost three feet. But was it enough to be out of the line of fire? He looked around for something to throw.

"Here." Remi handed him an ink pen. "It was in my shirt pocket."

"Thanks." He tossed it past the left side of the table. Nothing.

He looked back at her. "Either we're out of his line of sight now or—"

"He wants us to think we are."

"Only one way to find out." He scrambled forward in a half crouch, half run, then dived past the table. *Boom! Boom!* The floor splintered inches from his right foot. He swore and rolled toward the fireplace, then scooted back against the wall of stone that formed the floor-to-ceiling chimney and hearth.

Remi cursed even more than he had, blasting the shooter for his mean trick in making Duncan think he might be safe.

"I'm okay," he called out. "You can quit cursing."

She cursed some more, just to be ornery and leaned toward the couch to get a better view of him.

Keeping his back to the wall, careful to stay away from the still unbroken window on the left, he inched closer to the center of the fireplace. Then he jumped up on the hearth and grabbed the gun from over the mantel, along with the box of ammo in the decorative wood box beneath it. After loading the rifle, he jumped down, apparently considering his next move.

She considered his options, too. If she was in his position, there was probably only one thing to do. Make a run for it. The only question was which direction—left or right? The shooter had obviously seen him sprint from behind the coffee table. The stacked-stone chimney above the roofline made it clear that he had to be by the fireplace. Had the shooter moved to another vantage point where he'd have an angle at the other window? The shooter had to be in a tree. Moving to another tree would require that he climb down, then up the next one. That would take time. Duncan must have come to the same conclusion, because his hand tightened around the rifle and he looked toward her. His brows drew down.

"Remi. You need to back up farther behind the table. And stay here. You promised."

"Technically, I didn't *promise* anything."

"Remi—"

"Just hurry and get him, okay? I don't even have my cell phone to call for backup. The battery's dead."

"Yeah, well, don't beat yourself up. Mine's charged, but it's sitting on the kitchen table, where it's doing us absolutely no good."

She swore again.

He grinned. "I'll be back in time for dinner, honey." He shoved some extra shells in his pocket.

"You'd better be. Stay safe, Duncan. I can't... I don't..."

His expression softened. "Tell me all about it when I get back." He gripped his rifle in his right hand and took off for the front door.

A rifle cracked behind him. Glass shattered. He threw the dead bolt and lunged out the door.

REMI DUCKED, COVERING her head and drawing her legs up to her chest as more rifle fire seemed to explode around her. She'd heard the sound of Duncan diving to the ground outside while the shooter fired shots through the window on the other side of the fireplace. But the angle was all wrong. Slivers of wood kicked up from the log walls on the other side of the room, well above the floor. The shooter must have been climbing down the tree, or maybe he'd moved to another one while Duncan was getting his gun.

Either way, he hadn't been high enough to get a bead on Duncan when he'd run for the door. Which was good and bad. Good because he'd missed Duncan. Bad because he was lower to the ground now and had to know Duncan was coming after him. Bad guy with a gun was likely on the ground now, too, and positioning himself for an ambush.

She couldn't just lie there and hope Duncan had thought about the same thing. She needed to get her gun and back him up. With her right hand out of commission, even if she'd had the benefit of a long gun, she'd have zero accuracy. But accuracy wasn't what he needed from her. He needed a distraction, a diversion.

Using the same trick that Duncan had, she grabbed some shards of wood and glass off the floor and tossed them in the air. Nothing. She tried again. Still nothing. Hoping that meant the shooter wasn't looking through his scope at her position and waiting for her to appear, she pushed herself to her feet. The pain from her right shoulder was blinding. Black spots swam in front of her eyes. She drew deep breaths, forcing oxygen into her lungs. Her vision cleared.

She was going to have to tie her arm tightly into place so she could stand the pain without passing out. For now, though, she settled for clasping her right arm with her left.

If the gunman had been watching, he'd have had a perfectly clear shot at her. No way could she squirm and drop and roll like Duncan had. But no bullets came flying through the window. She drew a ragged breath and ran for the kitchen. She made it through the archway and swiped Duncan's cell phone off the table, biting her lip at the pain in her shoulder when she let her bad arm go. Then she ran into the back hall.

She'd just made it to the bedroom when she dropped to her knees. The phone fell from her hand and she grasped her hurt shoulder. Hot tears were streaming down her cheeks. The pain was worse than before. If she survived this day she'd probably end up having surgery, and be lucky if she ever regained full use of the thing. That thought had her burning mad and up on her feet again. The psychopath outside had taken everything from her, including possibly the use of her right arm. No way was he going to take Duncan, too.

She grabbed the phone, but the home screen was locked. Without Duncan's pass code she couldn't call for backup.

Boom! Bam!

Two different guns fired outside. If she was going to help him, she needed to get out there. Now!

She put her sling on and brutally tightened it to immobilize her arm against her chest. Then she shoved Duncan's phone in her pocket and grabbed her pistol out of the nightstand drawer. Loading a magazine was awkward but she managed to balance it between the bed and her thigh and jam the gun down on top of it, locking it in place.

She ran for the back door. She didn't even stop to look for either man. She flew past the hot tub and bolted down the stairs to the backyard. Then she stopped, aiming her pistol toward the trees as she used the deck stairs for cover. Nothing. Where was the gunman? Where was Duncan?

Whack. Smack. Crack.

She didn't know what those sounds were, but she took off running toward them, assuming they had to have come from at least one of the men. She rounded a copse of pines and slid to a halt on some dried up pine needles.

Duncan stood ten feet away, his chest heaving from exertion. And at his feet, his neck twisted at an impossible angle, lay the gunman, his sightless eyes staring up at the canopy of tree branches overhead.

She ran to Duncan, barreling into him and wrapping her good arm around his waist. He grunted from the impact, then steadied himself and put his arms around her.

"It's okay," he whispered against the top of her head. "It's okay. It's over."

She squeezed him, hard, then pulled back, wincing at the tug of pain in her right shoulder. "You're okay? He didn't shoot you, did he?"

"I'm okay. He ran out of ammo and charged me. I could have shot him. But he just looked so…young. I tried to give him a chance. But he pulled a knife. I didn't have a choice." He frowned down at her. "I told you to wait in the cabin."

"Yeah, well. I've never been good at following orders. And I wasn't going to lie there waiting to be rescued when someone was trying to kill you."

He looked at the pistol still in her left hand, pointing at the ground, and his face paled. "Aren't you right-handed?"

She shoved the gun in her pocket. "I figured I could create a diversion, if nothing else."

He scrubbed his face and shook his head. "Thank goodness it didn't come to that."

She grinned, feeling lighthearted in knowing that the ordeal was finally over. "I was going to call for backup. But I didn't know your code to unlock your phone." She handed it to him and he slid it into his pocket, looking too drained to make a call just yet. She understood the feeling. Everything had happened so fast, too fast. The world felt off-kilter, just plain… off. They both needed to catch their breath.

Still smiling, she finally looked down to see whether she knew the shooter. She stopped smiling. An older, harder-looking Billy Hendricks lay on his back, his rifle a few feet away, where it must have landed when he'd realized he was out of ammo. All these years she thought she was searching for a stranger, when the man who'd killed her sister was someone she'd known.

Duncan put an arm around her waist, as careful as ever not to jar her shoulder. "Don't look at him. Don't let him hurt you anymore. It's over."

She forced her gaze away. "I know. It just feels… surreal. Strange. All these years I thought Billy was just one of us, someone who knew Becca. He even posted on her page, the website my dad put up, saying he was praying for us." She shivered, and it had nothing to do with the chilly air and the fact that she wasn't wearing her jacket. "And all along, he was the one who'd taken her from us."

"It's freezing out here. Why don't you head up to the house and warm up in front of the fire?" he said. "I'll be up in a few minutes, right after I call this in and get the crime scene guys on their way. Then I'm taking you to the hospital. No arguing this time."

"Don't worry. I won't argue. I want some really good drugs and I don't know any dealers around here." She grinned, and then headed toward the house.

DUNCAN WAITED UNTIL she was out of sight before sliding down to the ground and resting his back against a pine tree. Feeling unbelievably weary, he pulled out his cell phone, and placed the call to his boss. He turned on the speaker function and set the phone on a nearby rock. Then he yanked off one of his socks and held it against his lower left side, putting pressure on the laceration that Billy had made before Duncan was able to disarm him.

Chapter Fifteen

"Enough with the fifty questions," Duncan said over the phone. "I'm freezing out here. When will the crime scene techs arrive? I can't stand guard duty all afternoon and night, keeping wild animals off the perp." He frowned at the blood-soaked sock and tossed it to the ground. He tugged his other sock off and pressed that to his side. He was glad that Remi had listened to him, for once, and went to the house to warm up. But, also knowing her, he was mildly surprised she hadn't thought to come back with a jacket for him. Then again, she hadn't realized he planned on waiting out here for the techs this long.

"They should be there in a few more minutes."

"Good." He pulled the sock away and swore.

"Duncan. What's wrong?"

"Nothing a few stitches won't cure. The perp stuck me with his knife before I got him in a headlock. The stupid wound won't quit bleeding."

His boss swore enough for both of them. "Why didn't you tell me you were wounded? Hold on."

Duncan closed his eyes and pressed the bloody

sock against his side as he listened to his boss order one of the others to get an ambulance to his house.

"They're ten minutes out. How bad is it?"

"Apparently worse than I thought. I'm getting woozy."

"That may be the only thing that saves you from my wrath. Blood loss might excuse your poor judgment."

Duncan figured the fact that he was slowly freezing to death could also help explain why his brain wasn't firing on all pistons. He should have told his boss right away that he needed a medic. But Lee had fired off so many questions he'd been too busy answering them to realize how badly he was bleeding. The stupid thing wouldn't stop no matter how hard he pressed.

"Did the suspect have any ID on him?" Lee asked. "And if you haven't already checked, don't do it now. Just be still and keep pressure on the wound."

"I don't have to check. I recognize him from pictures I saw while Remi and I were researching the case earlier. It's Billy Hendricks, from Colorado originally. He went to high school with Remi and her sister."

"Billy Hendricks? Are you sure?"

Duncan glanced at the dead man's face, the same face he'd seen standing behind Remi and Becca in the hallway of their school, looking like he wanted to murder Becca. And then, later, he had. "It's Hendricks. I'm sure. He had an alibi for Becca's murder, said he was with another girl, Felicia Reynolds, that night. But she admitted today that she lied to cover for him."

"Did she tell you why?"

"Something about believing he was too nice to do something like that, so she wanted to protect him. She was sweet on him at the time."

"Maybe she doesn't know the whole truth then and really just thought she was helping him out. In reality, she was just giving him a cover to use with the chaperones."

Duncan frowned. "What are you talking about?"

"The BAU has been looking, and I mean looking hard, into the backgrounds of all the men who were on that senior class trip, including Billy Hendricks. The night that Becca Jordan disappeared, Hendricks was an hour away using a fake ID to drink and gamble at Harrah's Cherokee Casino."

"Harrah's. Are you sure? That never came up in any of the reports, not even Pops's informal file he kept on the investigation."

"You can blame the almighty tourism dollar and politics for that little jewel. The FBI had a separate report they didn't include in the file that they shared with our office back then. Apparently, when they interviewed Hendricks he confessed to sneaking into the casino. Video confirmed he was there and couldn't have abducted Miss Jordan. But having an underage kid get past their security could have jeopardized their liquor license and caused them embarrassment on top of that. The mayor of Gatlinburg at the time stepped in with the FBI and convinced them to keep the casino jaunt a secret. The FBI knew Hendricks wasn't their guy, so they really didn't care if the casino and mayor wanted to keep things quiet and not damage the casino's reputation or endanger its liquor license. Bottom line, there's just no way that Billy Hendricks abducted Becca Jordan."

Duncan frowned. "That doesn't make sense. If Billy didn't kill Becca, then why would he come here and try to kill Remi? It made sense in a psychopathic kind of way that if he killed one twin and saw the other one later, he'd want to kill her, too."

"I don't know. It's too bad that he has an ironclad alibi for Becca's disappearance, because he *doesn't* have an alibi for Sheryl Foster's. Not that we've been able to find, at least. He's a long-haul trucker and had a delivery in this area the night before she was abducted. He doesn't have another haul scheduled for several days. The FBI obtained video from a local gas station that showed his rig driving through town and out toward the park the night before Foster disappeared. They haven't found that rig on any other video since then. That leads me to believe he'd holed up somewhere nearby, and was doing his best to stay out of sight. My guess is we'll find his rig, which is just the cab since he delivered the trailer he was hauling, somewhere close to your cabin, maybe parked at one of the rentals that tend to be vacant this time of year."

Duncan was having a hard time wrapping his mind around what he was hearing about Billy. The guy didn't abduct Becca. But he could have abducted Foster. And he'd tried to kill Remi. Why would he do that unless he was involved in her sister's disappearance somehow? If Billy had been Becca's killer, then it made a sick kind of sense that he'd wanted to kill the other twin, too. It even seemed reasonable that he'd come here because he was worried that Remi was onto him and would figure out he'd murdered her sister. But since he wasn't the killer, why attack Remi? There was no motivation for him to be here. It couldn't be a random coincidence.

One blonde. One brunette.

Two different types of victims.

Billy had an alibi for one victim, but not the other.

Duncan's blood ran cold in his veins. His hand tightened on the phone.

"Lee, you said the FBI is looking into the alibis of the men who participated in that senior trip. What about alibis for the other abductions and killings at other parks? What did they find out about Hendricks?"

"Give me a minute."

Duncan heard the sound of papers shuffling.

"Okay, got it. Lots of stuff to check out, but so far Hendricks has alibis for a handful of the cases and doesn't have any verifiable alibi for the others."

"Which ones does he not have alibis for? What do those victims have in common?" He waited. "Lee?"

"Blond. The ones we can't verify his alibi for are the blonde victims."

"And he alibis out for the brunettes?"

"So far, it's looking that way."

Billy didn't kill Becca.

But he could have killed Foster.

Two different victims.

One blonde. One brunette.

Duncan's gaze shot toward the cabin. "Two killers. Why didn't I see it? One prefers blondes, the other brunettes. Billy had a partner. He kills the blondes. His partner takes the brunettes." He was about to hang up on his boss to call Remi and warn her. Then he remembered that her cell phone battery was dead.

He swore and shoved himself to his feet, then fell against the tree. He swore again, wobbled back to standing, then swiped the cell phone from where it had fallen and took off through the trees.

"Remi!" he yelled as soon as he cleared the tree line. The shattered windows on the back of the house were like gaping maws mocking him with the silence behind them. "Remi!"

"What's going on?" Lee demanded.

"Two killers," he repeated, between gasping breaths as he jogged up the steep incline. "Someone's working with Billy. Someone he's known a long time, maybe even since high school. They're tag-teaming. Billy kills the blondes. His partner kills the brunettes."

"But if Billy killed Foster, didn't he already get his blonde? Why go after Remi? She's blond. What about that whole constellation thing?"

"She's a natural brunette. She dyed her hair for this case. Billy knew Becca and Remi. He knew she wasn't a true blonde. And so would his partner. If Billy was on the ridge staking out Foster when he saw Remi, he might have gotten confused, thinking he was seeing Becca again, except as a blonde." He reached the bottom of the stairs and fell to his knees. He was dizzy. Had to draw a deep breath. Forced his feet back under him and bounded up the stairs.

"Why take Foster at all then? Why not just take Remi as his blonde victim?"

"Because Vale and then I showed up and messed up his game. Billy took Foster as a substitute. We already know they go off script, kill others, based on what you found in the cave. Remi was too tempting to pass up. She was the one who got away. That's why Billy came here. Or maybe he was worried his partner would go after Remi because she's a natural brunette, and he wanted to beat him to it, because she was Becca's twin. Maybe he felt territorial. Who knows how these sick minds work?"

"It all makes sense in a macabre way. Where is she?"

Duncan tried to throw open the sliding glass door. It was locked. He ran to the right and leaped through the opening where one of the picture windows had been. "Remi! Remi!" He sprinted through the kitchen to the back hall, into his bedroom.

"Duncan, report. Where is Special Agent Jordan?"

He rushed to the other bedroom, checked both bathrooms, vaulted down the stairs to the basement level. Nothing, nothing, nothing. He hurried back upstairs and burst out the front door. He didn't stop until he was standing in the middle of the road, looking all around as he turned in a circle.

"Where is she?" his boss asked again.

"Gone." Duncan forced the word past his tight throat. "Remi's gone."

Chapter Sixteen

Remi kicked at the taillight from inside the trunk once again, twice, then collapsed back in exhaustion. She knew all the tricks for getting out of a locked trunk, like pulling the emergency release.

There wasn't one.

Or breaking the back seat so she could get out that way.

There was a piece of steel at the back of the trunk, no way to even reach the seat.

Or shatter the taillight and stick something through the hole, like her foot or her hand, so passersby would see it and call the police.

Whoever had knocked her out and abducted her from Duncan's house had put a wire mesh cover over the lights, making it impossible for her to break them no matter how hard she tried.

The only good thing was that whatever her captor had used to drug her had the side effect of numbing her shoulder. Otherwise, bumping around in the trunk would likely have had her writhing with pain.

How long had she been riding around in this

trunk? Since she'd been unconscious for part of the journey, she couldn't be sure. Ten minutes? Thirty? An hour? Whoever had abducted her had to know the cabin belonged to a federal officer. The Jeep parked out front with its NPS shield was a huge giveaway. Was the driver meandering around town to make sure no one was following him? Had he stopped some-where and hid out for a bit, while she was still asleep, making sure there wasn't any traffic before he pulled out again? All those questions were running through her mind without any answers, and one overriding thought kept repeating itself.

I'm going to die.

Duncan's face swam in her mind's eye. Duncan. At least he was safe. She didn't have to worry about him being in the middle of this, whatever this was. What an unexpected, wonderful bright spot in her life to have met him. She just hoped he wouldn't blame himself for whatever happened to her. It wasn't his fault. It was this jerk's fault who'd captured her.

I'm going to die.

Probably, yes. Most likely. But she wouldn't go easily. She might be small, and injured, but she still had her wits, plus fingernails and, luckily, shoes on her feet, so she could scratch and kick him. And she could run. Miles and miles. All she needed was the element of surprise, and she'd take off like a deer with a pack of wolves on its tail.

And if he caught her? Well, then she'd just have to figure out how to kill him, without getting herself killed. Because she hadn't spent her entire adult life locking animals like him up only to die at the hands of one. Somehow, she'd figure a way out of this.

The car slowed, then turned right and started up an incline. The road was curvy, tilting her from side to side, but she braced herself to keep from falling over. A few minutes later, the car slowed again, then braked hard and turned right, throwing her against the side of the trunk. She sucked in a sharp breath at the resulting burn in her shoulder muscles. The drugs were starting to wear off.

She tilted her body in the other direction, taking the pressure off her shoulder. The car started bouncing up and down and side to side. Something scraped the roof with a metallic scratching sound. Something else scraped along the left side. She gritted her teeth against the fiery pain in her shoulder, not to mention every other joint in her bruised and battered body. A little while later, a loud rushing sound filled the air. A waterfall. Not a large one, but there was no mistaking that sound.

They were back in the mountains.

DUNCAN LIFTED HIS head from the examining room table to look at Lee. "Did the guys find any trace of—"

Thunk. The doctor shoved his head back down. Again.

"Hey," Duncan complained, glaring at him. "Would you stop doing that?"

"I'm trying to keep you from bleeding to death. Hold still so I can finish closing the wound."

The doctor jabbed the needle into his skin. Duncan automatically jerked from the motion, but thankfully, his side had been numbed. He narrowed his eyes at the doctor, figuring he'd done that on purpose.

"Just be still," Lee said, drawing closer to the table. "You're in no shape to join any search parties, anyway. The best way for you to help Special Agent Jordan is to use that brain of yours to help us figure out who has her and where he's taken her."

Duncan glared at the doctor again. "I'm perfectly fine. They're loading me up with IV fluids. I just need Dr. Jekyll here to finish his stitches. Sometime today would be nice."

The man shook his head and kept sewing.

Lee leaned over Duncan. "That's a nasty cut. Looks like a shark took a bite out of your side. You're really lucky you didn't bleed out before the ambulance got there."

The doctor snipped the thread and paused with his needle in the air. "Yes, he is. Extremely lucky. But next time, ask for another doctor." He tossed his garbage in the medical waste container and stalked out without another word.

Duncan grimaced as Lee helped him sit up. "Guess I owe him an apology. But he was so slow. He knew I'm in the middle of a case and needed to get out of here fast." He reached for his shirt at the foot of the table, then grimaced again, seeing the blood all over it.

Lee snatched it and tossed it in the trash. "You can't put that back on. Civilians would see all that blood and call 911, thinking an ax murderer was on the loose. I'll get one of the guys to bring you a shirt from one of their go-bags."

Duncan gave him a droll look. "Really? Whose shirt's gonna fit me?"

Lee frowned. "What did your mama feed you and your brothers growing up? Whole hogs?"

Duncan rolled his eyes and hopped down from the table. He looked around, then grabbed a hospital gown and yanked it on. "This will do for now. Maybe you can get a couple of the guys to drive my Jeep here. I've got a go-bag with extra clothes inside."

"Will do."

"Which room is Vale in?" Duncan asked, as he strode into the hallway. "I only spoke to him on the phone before. I want to talk to him again, show him Billy's picture, see if he remembers anything else that might help us figure out a description of whoever has Remi, if nothing else."

"Vale's not here," Lee said. "I thought the same thing as you when I got here. I had one of the other guys go ask him if I could interview him. But he's gone."

Duncan stopped and turned. "What do you mean, gone? He nearly bled out a couple of days ago."

"So did you, less than an hour ago. And yet here you are, all stitched up and running around."

"I was slashed, not stabbed. Vale was shot. Big difference. No way should he have been released yet." He headed to the information desk, flashed his badge, and a few moments later had the information he needed. He headed back toward Lee and passed him on his way down the hall. "Tell me everything you know about Vale," he called over his shoulder.

Lee rushed to catch up to him. "Okay, but where are you going in such an all-fired hurry."

"I know the guy who runs security here. I've worked with him many times on other cases."

"Again, why?"

Duncan paused outside the security office. "Because Vale left the hospital against medical advice. And he'd told me over the phone he had no interest in bringing charges against Remi, or suing, even though he probably could have gotten a lot of money if he had. Could be nothing, but could be something."

"What, you're thinking Vale is our other guy, Billy's partner?"

"Maybe. Maybe not. But I know one thing. Vale had plenty of time to leave the hospital and get to my place and grab Remi. And I also know that Remi was convinced he had a gun up on that ridge."

"But we never found one."

"Doesn't mean he didn't have one. He could have thrown it when I was handcuffing Remi, just like she said."

"You're reaching."

He whirled around. "I'm desperate. And I've learned a lot about Remi. She's smart, and honest. If she says he had a gun, that's good enough for me. I just want to do one thing. Find out if he had any visitors while he was here, and if so, whether Billy was one of them."

Twenty minutes later, a grainy image from a hallway camera came up in the security office, showing a familiar man walking to Vale's hospital room.

"Billy," Duncan and Lee said at the same time.

"And he brought a bag. Clothes, maybe? For Vale?" Lee wondered.

"Just this morning," Duncan added. "I bet he came to tell Vale he was going after Remi. But Vale wanted her for himself. So after Billy left, Vale decided to go after him, maybe to stop him, or maybe just to claim Remi as his next victim."

As they watched the recording being fast-forwarded, Lee got a call. He quickly took it, then hung up, looking pale.

Duncan's mouth went dry. He couldn't even bring himself to ask. He just waited.

"It's not Remi," Lee rushed to assure him. "That was Pops. He was with a crew I sent back to the ridge, looking for any fresh signs that someone might have gone that way again. He found a gun, about forty feet into the woods from where you performed first aid on Vale."

"What kind of gun?" Duncan demanded.

"Glock 19, 9 mm."

Duncan swore. "I never should have doubted her. If I'd listened, really listened, I could have—"

"What? Arrested the guy she shot? The victim? Her story didn't hold water at the time. Hindsight is twenty-twenty. You can't blame yourself. Besides, we don't know for sure that Vale is involved. He may have had a gun like her, for protection, and didn't want to get in trouble so he tossed it."

"You believe that?"

"I believe the facts. And those are pretty slim pickings right now."

"Here you go," Duncan's friend said. "He's coming out of the room, ten minutes after he went in."

Duncan and Lee stared at the screen. Billy stepped out of Vale's room, no longer carrying the bag. And beside him, fully dressed, was Vale. They both walked down the hall and got into the elevator.

"Son of a—" Lee began.

"Vale's our guy," Duncan said. "We need to get a BOLO out right away on him. And we need to figure out what he's driving, what he does for a living, how he got here and where he may be holed up. And we need to find out all of that yesterday."

THE SUDDEN CESSATION of movement bothered Remi more than all the bouncing that had made her shoulder throb with pain. Her captor had stopped the car. Which meant they were wherever he planned to take her, and that he was about to get on with it, do whatever he planned to do to her.

She twisted around, positioning her feet toward the rear bumper. He'd taken away her sling and zip-tied her hands together, in front of her. And he hadn't bound her legs. So she had at least those two things going for her. If she could surprise him when he opened the trunk, she could kick out at him, throw him off balance and then throw herself out of the car. Then she could take off running.

The car shook. A door slammed. Shoes crunched against the ground as he rounded the vehicle, coming toward the back.

She scooted closer to the bumper side, lifted her knees higher.

Click. The trunk sprang up. Something dark loomed in front of her.

She kicked with all her strength. Her legs hit the dark shape, but it was like hitting nothing. Her body jerked forward with her momentum and she tumbled out of the trunk onto whatever she'd kicked. A tarp! He'd waved a tarp in front of her and she'd charged like a raging bull. He'd tricked her.

Laughter had her jerking around. A man stood over her, the sun behind him so she couldn't see his face. And he was too far away for her to kick him, even if she could. Her legs were tangled up in the heavy tarp. She desperately shuffled her feet, trying to get free.

"Your sister tried the same thing when I opened the trunk to get her out."

Remi froze and stared up at him. Becca? He was the one who'd taken Becca?

"She kicked me good. Hit me square in the jaw." He chuckled again. "But I've taken far worse than what she dished out. Still, I figured you might think like her, try that same trick. I was ready this time." He crouched down, the sun no longer obscuring his features, or the big serrated hunting knife in his right hand.

Remi sucked in a breath as recognition dawned.

"That's right." He grinned. "Kurt Vale, pleased to meet ya. But we met once before, didn't we? Up on that ridge. If it wasn't for my gun getting caught in my pocket, I'd have popped one off before you did." He tapped his side and winced. "And I wouldn't be sporting a bullet hole now. Then again, I'd have had to kill that stupid cop who showed up, and then the whole police force, local and Feds, would have rained down on me. I guess you did me a favor, in hindsight. Everyone thinks I'm the victim here." He laughed again. "What a trip, huh?"

"What did you do to my sister?" she demanded, eyeing the knife in his hand.

"Nothing she didn't want me to do. Not at first, anyway." He winked.

Remi's stomach clenched.

"Don't worry." He slid the knife into a leather holder strapped to his thigh. "I'm about to do you a favor right back. I'm about to answer all your questions, by showing you exactly what I did to your sister, in intimate detail. I figure it's only fair, don't you? You've been searching for her all these years. I think it's time you finally found her."

He waved toward the trees around them. "This is where I brought her that night, in the trunk of my car. Easy peasy, because she snuck out of camp to meet me, following the instructions in my note to keep to the hard rocky parts of the trail so she wouldn't leave any footprints for a nosy chaperone to follow."

"You're lying." Remi very slowly moved her legs, trying to slide them out from the tarp so she could make a break for it. "She didn't even know you. She wouldn't have gone to meet with you."

"True. She didn't know me, even though I'd seen her from afar. I was a friend of Billy's, a year younger. You didn't realize that, did you? He was tired of Becca snubbing him and asked me to join him on the senior trip to teach her a lesson. So that's what I did, followed the buses up here and set up camp out in the woods. Billy gave her that note. I waited. And out came beautiful Becca, right into my arms."

"Liar." Remi's right foot was free. She pulled the fabric toward her with her left hand, slowly, and sought to keep him distracted as she tried to free her left foot. "She wouldn't have gone to meet Billy, either."

He cocked his head. "Well, now. Who said anything about her meeting Billy? That Garrett fellow was who she was sweet on, Garrett Weber. Popular guy in school. Total wuss. Lived down the street from me. But the girls liked him well enough. When Becca read that note saying he'd dumped his girlfriend because he wanted her instead, she couldn't get out of camp fast enough."

Oh, Becca. Grief shot through Remi, but she tamped it down. Her left foot slid free. *Now.*

She yanked the tarp up and threw it over his head.

He let out a guttural yell, cursing at her as he grabbed at the cloth.

She scrambled to her feet and bolted for the woods.

Chapter Seventeen

Duncan tucked his shirt into his jeans, glad to ditch the hospital gown now that a couple of his peers had driven his Jeep to the NPS trailer and brought him his go-bag. He thanked them, then leaned over the enormous table in the middle of the office, a black Sharpie in his hand as he looked at the map of the Great Smoky Mountains National Park and surrounding area.

"Patterson, you said you searched grid eighteen?"

Patterson, one of the rangers on loan from Atlanta, gave him a thumbs-up from the other side of the room where he was getting coffee.

Duncan circled the grid, wrote Patterson's name and placed a black checkmark beside it.

"Pops, where did your team search?" he called out.

"You don't have to yell. I'm right beside you, son."

"Oh, sorry." Duncan scrubbed his face. It had been an hour since he'd left the hospital, two since Remi had been taken. Where was she?

"We searched here." Pops pointed to the map. "And

here. Just finished that one. What area do you want me to try next?"

Lee had been talking to some other investigators and searchers, and came over to stand beside Pops. "I've got crews in five grids in the park right now." He took Duncan's pen and circled those. "Gatlinburg PD has roadblocks in and out of town. We've got roadblocks on every major route in and out of the area."

Duncan shook his head. "It's taking too long. We'd need thousands to search the whole park. And we all know we can't block every potential access point. The area's just too big." He tossed his pen down. "Has the BAU told you anything useful about Vale yet?"

Lee shrugged. "Just what we learned thirty minutes ago on the last status call. That he's a long-haul trucker, like his buddy Hendricks was. Different companies, but similar routes. Vale grew up in Colorado, went to the same high school. Got in trouble a lot, spent time in detention, which is where we figure he first met Billy."

"They must have been friends back during the senior trip, ten years ago," Duncan said. "Vale either followed the class up here, planning on mischief, or was here before they arrived. Either way, he and Billy likely planned the attack on Becca. That whole casino visit was probably to give Billy an alibi. Meanwhile no one even realized Vale was around."

Pops thumped the map. "Unless you come up with a better plan, I'm going to take my men over by the Sugarlands Visitor Center and see if we can find anyone who saw Vale in the likely time frame if he did come back to the park with Special Agent Jordan."

"Oh, he came back, all right," Duncan said. "This is a game for him. It started with her sister here in the park. He toyed with Remi with that skeleton. He's going to finish it here, too."

Pops grasped his shoulder in a tight squeeze. "We'll find her. Black Charger, right? The car that's registered to Vale?"

"Colorado plates." He rattled off the number, which he already knew by heart. "Don't forget to ask about Hendricks's rig. It's a white Freightliner with Colorado plates, too. We didn't find it near my cabin. Vale may have taken the rig instead of his car."

"You got it." Pops grabbed his coat and headed out the door with a handful of rangers.

Lee marked the visitor's center on the map, along with Pops's name.

Duncan looked around. There were a dozen people on the phones, on computers, looking at maps, and dozens more out in the field. But no one had scared up even one report of a black Charger or white semi-truck cab near his cabin or near the park today. So how had Vale gotten away from his house with Remi, without a single neighbor on that long road remembering either of those vehicles?

"What's going on in that head of yours?" Lee said.

"Vale. Obviously he drove Remi out of the area and then likely drove her up here, to the park some-where. But no one near my cabin saw a semitruck or a Charger. I don't exactly live in a subdivision with a neighborhood watch group. But there are plenty of cabins nearby and that's a fairly busy main road to that particular area. Someone at a gas station at the bottom of the mountain, or a restaurant, or a store, had to have seen something. You pulled all closed-circuit surveillance video in the area?"

"I pulled everything within a five mile radius. There wasn't one single semi up on that mountain in the time frame that we need. There were two black Chargers, both with local plates. Both were ruled out. Gatlinburg PD tracked down the owners."

Duncan dropped his head, his hands braced against the table. "Think, think, think. What am I missing? He couldn't have physically hauled her through the woods. Our team would have found evidence of that. And there's just nowhere to go up there. He had to drive out. She was tied up either in the back seat or in the trunk. But he had to have her in a vehicle. All that video footage, did the police look for Vale, specifically, as the driver? I think we can narrow it down to a car, something with a trunk or back seat where no one would see Remi."

"They're not amateurs. I'm sure they looked at every vehicle that passed any business with a camera with a view of the street. And before you ask, no, there's no point of entry up on that mountain where you live that isn't covered by a camera. The police were thorough, looking at every driver of every car and truck that came through. It's like the two of them just disappeared, or flew out in a helicopter or something." He snorted, without amusement.

Duncan frowned, Lee's words running through his head. "How's the neighborhood canvassing going?"

"Every house, RV, shed, hell, even hot tubs within a few miles of your place have been searched. She's not up there, Duncan."

He closed his eyes, his arms still braced on the table. Vale and Remi had come down from the mountain. There was only one road he could have used. Cameras would show every vehicle going up or down. So how could Vale drive right past them and the police not realize it was him?

He jerked his head up. "A police car. Vale's got a police car, or an NPS vehicle. Something official that the police wouldn't look twice at when they were scanning the video. Tell them to look again, but this time look for something official, not a civilian vehicle."

Lee already had his phone out. While he spoke to Gatlinburg PD, Duncan studied the map of the area closest to his house. He was making a huge assumption that Vale would risk coming back into the park. But he also knew about killers' signatures, and how important it was to a serial killer to complete his ritual. Which meant Vale had to bring Remi here. But where, in over a quarter of a million acres, would he take her? Again, logically, it seemed like he'd take her back to the ridge where Foster had been taken. But that place had been searched twice today already. So where was he?

He put X's by the roads that led up the mountain near the ridge, where Becca had disappeared all those years ago. There were four roads to that area, not counting the one that passed in front of the NPS trailer, which wasn't a road civilians used.

Duncan grew still, looking at the map. A road to the area near the senior class campsite, that few people traveled, would be extremely tempting to someone like Vale. In fact, it would be perfect.

Lee ended his call, his face grim. "You were right. A police car headed down the mountain within five minutes of you calling me from your cabin to report that Hendricks had been killed. And the officer who uses that car can't be reached. They're sending patrol to his house now."

"Where's his house?" Duncan asked, even though he was fairly certain he already knew the answer.

"Same mountain as you. About a mile away."

"Put a BOLO out—"

"Gatlinburg PD's already got that handled. They'll contact businesses with cameras along the main road leading from where they saw that police car and track its movements, figure out where it went." He rattled off the car number. "I'll get all my guys searching for that police cruiser. We'll check our own video around the park entrances, see if it came up one of the main roads."

Duncan strode toward the door.

"Where are you going?"

"To search the road out front. It's the most likely place he would have gone." Duncan grabbed his coat and gloves off the pegs on the wall.

"Duncan, stop," Lee called after him. "You're in no condition to—"

He let the door close on his boss's words and took off in a run toward his Jeep.

HE WAS HERDING HER, like a border collie forcing a lost lamb back to the other sheep, and she couldn't do a dang thing about it. There was simply nowhere else to go. His crashing footfalls pounded after her in the brush, that irritating laughter floating to her in the breeze. He was making no attempt to hide where he was and didn't have to. She'd made the mistake of following the trail where the road ended, thinking it would be easier to run full out that way and escape. But the killer knew these woods better than her. He knew the path ran along some cliffs, with steep drops onto sharp rocks below. As soon as she'd reached the cliffs, she'd jerked around to head back, to try to thread her way through the woods somewhere else. And he'd been right there, grinning at her, holding that impossibly long, jagged-edged knife that looked like a close cousin to a machete.

She'd shivered, bile rising in her throat. She didn't want to die. And she really didn't want to get hacked to death.

"This is exactly what Becca did," he'd said, laughing again. "She ran down the path, just like you. You're making this too easy!"

She'd taken off running, with him loping after her.

Help me, Becca. Where did you go? Where should I not go?

She glanced around, desperate for a break in the trees, somewhere to hide. But the rock face of the mountain loomed on her right, the steep drop-off to her left.

Maybe where the trail curved up ahead there would be somewhere to hide, a way to ambush him. It was her only hope right now. Clasping her hurt arm against her chest, she put on a fresh burst of speed.

DUNCAN SWORE AND turned the Jeep around at the field with the cell tower. He'd gone down the mountain first, to the parking lot where he'd once taken Remi to get her purse out of her car. The lot was empty. He'd driven around the perimeter, just in case Vale had pulled the stolen police car just inside the tree line. But there was nowhere for him to go. The trees were too thick in this section. Even an ATV couldn't get through here. He'd headed back up the mountain, all the way to the top, to the field where he'd once parked in order to see where Sheryl Foster had been abducted. Again, nothing.

He headed back down for another sweep of the road, going slowly as he thought through everything. He'd just passed the opening to the gravel parking lot and the NPS trailer when the radio in his glove box squawked. He grabbed it and clicked to respond.

"Duncan here."

"It's Lee. Where are you?"

"Just east of the NPS trailer entrance. Why?"

"A camera at the trailhead at the bottom of our access road picked up the stolen police car heading up there about half an hour ago. They're still scanning through additional video, but so far, they haven't seen it come out. Duncan, he's on our road somewhere. Has to be."

He slammed his brakes. He'd just passed the bird-watching trail where he'd parked to talk to Remi. If Vale had come up this way, maybe he'd turned down that same trail. It was worth a look.

He shifted into Reverse and zipped back to the entrance. Sure enough, fresh tire tracks dug into the damp grass where snow had been earlier, but had since melted. And the grass just past that was flattened from a recent passing.

"He's on the old bird-watching trail, two miles west of NPS. I'm going in."

"Wait, I don't even know what that is. What are you talking about?"

"It used to be a road, years ago. Then it was used as a trail, but it was deemed too dangerous and closed after that. Ask Pops. He's the one who showed it to me when he was teaching me the area. Two miles down the mountain, then head south."

Lee yelled at some of the rangers to grab their coats. "Stay put. We're coming to you."

"No time." He tossed the radio onto the seat beside him and slammed the accelerator.

REMI STOPPED AND bent over at the waist, panting, desperately trying to pull oxygen into her starved lungs. The distance she'd run wasn't great. But it had been over harsh terrain. Adrenaline was pumping through her body, and she'd been running at full speed rather than the slower pace of a cross-country runner. Her side ached. Her thighs were burning. Her arm was screaming at her. Constant pain and fear combined to steal her stamina and threatened to leave her lying on the ground, quivering like a beached jellyfish.

"Oh, *Reeemiiii*... I'm coming for you, darling."

The sickening sound of Vale's taunting had her jerking upright. The man wasn't human. He never seemed to stop to rest. He just kept coming.

The sound of steel scraping against the rock wall of the mountain that trapped her in on one side had her whimpering.

"I hear you, Remi! I hear you!"

She'd never hated anyone so much in her life. She drew a ragged breath and started running again. She'd just rounded the latest curve in the dangerously narrowing trail when it opened into a wide clearing. There were trees to her right, and a gray, weathered structure directly in front of her. She hesitated, not sure what to do. Try for the trees? Hope the rocky face of the mountain didn't continue around to the right and block her in again? Or head into the structure and hope she could find something to use to defend herself?

What did you do, Becca? Help me make the right decision.

Shoes skittered on rocks. He was coming up fast, just past the last curve in the trail.

What would Becca have done?

Remi made her decision, and heaved herself forward.

DUNCAN SLAMMED THE brakes and wrestled the steering wheel, bringing the Jeep to a teeth-grinding halt just inches from the police car. Vale had turned it sideways at the end of this section of trail, where it widened into a clearing before continuing again on the other side through the trees. He'd probably done it on purpose, either hoping to make a quick turnaround and getaway when he came back to the car, or blocking anyone who might come after him.

Duncan grabbed his radio and jumped out of the Jeep, aiming his gun at the police car as he ran to check inside. "Lee, come in. It's Duncan."

"We just found the trail. We're coming up."

"You're about ten minutes behind me. I found the police car." He rounded to the open trunk and wasn't surprised to find it empty. He frowned and leaned in close, then picked up a long blond hair from the carpet. Remi. He glanced around.

"The officer was killed," Lee announced. "Gatlinburg PD found him in a ditch, tossed like garbage. I've got three guys with me. I'll call for more now that we know we're on the right path. Wait there."

Duncan bent down, studying the footprints, figuring out what had happened based on the marks in the dirt. Then he took off running toward where the path continued beyond the clearing. "Can't wait. It looks like he had Remi in the trunk. She must have tried something. Maybe she hit him when he opened it. She has a mean left hook. He threw a tarp on her, probably intended to roll her up in it and carry her somewhere. But she got away, ran into the woods on the far side. I know this trail, Lee. It's a one-way ticket to the cliffs. No way out except to turn around. If I wait, she's as good as dead."

"Understood. Just don't get yourself killed, all right? I don't want to face those brothers of yours if you do."

He leaped over a fallen log, wincing at the feel of something tearing on his left side, probably his stitches.

Hang on, Remi. I'm coming. Just hang on.

He pounded through the woods, not even trying to be quiet. It didn't matter. In fact, he hoped Vale heard him. After all, he had a gun, and Remi didn't. Duncan knew where this trail ended, certain death with no safe hiding places if a murderer was chasing you. And Vale had a head start. Was he even now hurting Remi, using her in whatever sick fashion he'd used all the women he and Hendricks had abducted and killed over the years? Duncan had to do something, anything, to give her a fighting chance. He had to distract him, get Vale to go after him instead of Remi. And there was only one way to be absolutely certain the man heard him.

He raised his gun toward the sky and squeezed the trigger.

REMI JERKED AT the sound of a gunshot. So did Vale. He skidded to a halt in front of the dilapidated building, knife raised as he glanced over his shoulder.

Remi had been certain her sister would have rushed inside. So instead, she'd hurried around the right corner of the outside of the building, feeling terribly exposed. But she'd found a large rock, about six inches across, and she'd picked it up. She planned on bashing Vale's skull in when he went inside, searching for her. But as she carefully peered around the building at him, instead of going inside, now he stood in indecision.

Bam!

Another shot.

Vale grunted and turned around. He shoved his knife in its holder and reached down to his other ankle. He pulled out a Glock 19, just like the one he'd had at the ridge, and disappeared back down the path.

Remi stood frozen in shock. Vale had a gun all this time, could have mowed her down with a hail of bullets. But he'd wanted to stalk her instead, enjoy her fear. And now he was going after whoever had fired those shots.

The pain in her shoulder was suddenly too intense to ignore. She dropped the rock, her chest heaving as she leaned against the wall, holding her arm and trying to catch her breath. Whoever had fired those shots had given her some extra time, time to form a better plan if Vale came back. And she wasn't going to waste it.

She ran into the building to see if there was something she could use. It wasn't large, maybe twenty by twenty. It had been a barn or small house at one time, probably twice its current size. But the elements had taken their toll, shearing off the back half of the building and sweeping it down the cliff to the rocks below. Why someone had built the structure so close to the edge was beyond her. Then again, maybe a piece of the mountain had broken off over the years, making a once safe building now a perilously dangerous one. If someone ran straight through to the back, they'd fall out into space, then plummet to their death below.

Was that what happened to you, Becca? She prayed it wasn't, prayed that her sister hadn't suffered such unspeakable terror, knowing the whole time she was falling that she was going to die.

Bam!

Another shot sounded from outside, much closer than before.

"Vale!" a voice called out. "Come and get me, you sick fool!"

Duncan! That was Duncan's voice. What was he doing? Making himself a target to save her?

No. She couldn't lose him, not like this, not sacrificing himself for her. She had to help him. Somehow. She whirled around and ran back through the building. Then she skidded in the dirt and turned. What had she seen? Something had flashed at her as she'd run past. Was it something she could use to help him? She rushed back in and looked to her right, toward an old fireplace. There was something white, something... She rushed forward, then fell to her knees. Amid the ashes of a fire from long ago, lying over a wrought-iron grate, was what she'd been searching for for a decade.

Becca.

Her bones were covered with soot. Her once beautiful hair, what was left of it, lay in curly piles around her skull. And sticking out of her left femur was a lethal-looking steel pin, like a spike sticking out of the side of a club. It was the pin that had caught Remi's attention, somehow catching a ray of sunlight through one of the cracks in the ruined ceiling overhead.

Tears cascaded down onto her hand as she reached into the grate.

DUNCAN WOBBLED ON his feet, shaking his head to try to make both Vales turn back into one.

Vale chuckled. "Seeing stars, are ya now?" He circled in front of Duncan, his knife clutched menacingly in his right hand. "Me, I've never been one for astronomy or astrology or whatever it's called. But Billy, well, he was obsessed. All because of that stupid girl he wanted and could never have, Becca." He shook his head and gestured toward Duncan's side. "I don't know why I'm even bothering to toy with you. As much blood as you're losing, you're gonna pass out any minute now. No fun. Too easy."

"Give me back my gun if you think this is too easy."

Vale flashed a bright white smile. "If I'd wanted a gunfight I wouldn't have tossed both our guns after sneaking up on you. Still, yeah, I admit I might have been hasty. That's two guns you've cost me. And I aim to collect."

He suddenly charged at Duncan, knife raised.

Duncan leaped to the side and swept his foot around in a circle.

Vale went sprawling to the ground and did a face plant against an oak tree.

Duncan ran toward him to grab the knife, then jerked back just in time to avoid being stabbed as Vale jabbed it toward him.

Vale swore viciously and climbed laboriously to his feet, then wiped his mouth, glaring when his hand came away wet with blood. "You're gonna pay for that."

"Where's Remi?" Duncan asked, trying to buy time as they circled each other. All the while, he kept glancing around, looking for a stick, a big rock, anything he could use to give him an advantage. On any given day, he could have beat Vale, no problem. But he'd lost too much blood and was struggling just to keep from passing out. "Where is she?"

"Let's just say she's with her sister." He laughed again.

Duncan's heart sank. No, he couldn't believe this man. He was lying. Duncan had to believe that Remi was okay. Anything else was unthinkable.

They continued to circle. Vale lunged forward. Duncan leaped out of the way, the blade so close he could feel the cold air rushing around it as Vale swung it in a deadly arc.

"Put the knife down, Vale. It's not too late to try to cut a deal. Remi for your life. I could talk to the district attorney, get him to take the death penalty off the table if you give up and tell me where Remi is."

"Give up? I'm not the one bleeding to death here. And I'm the one with the knife. Have you lost your mind?"

"Did you think I came here alone?"

Vale's eyes widened. He looked at the trees around Duncan as if searching for others hiding behind him. "You're bluffing."

"Nope." Duncan pulled his radio out and hit the button. "Lee, how far out are you?"

Vale had started forward, but stopped when Lee answered. "A couple of minutes. We heard shots but you weren't answering."

"Had the volume down so it wouldn't distract me in our little fight here. Those were warning shots, from me to Vale. I don't have my gun anymore and he's got a knife. Come in hot. Shoot first. Ask questions later." He glared at Vale. "Kill the bastard." He tossed the radio to the ground.

Vale narrowed his eyes. "You just signed your death warrant." He let out a guttural yell and charged like a bull.

Duncan waited until Vale was almost on him before diving to the ground and whirling around with both hands clenched together, swinging his fists toward Vale's head. He hit him hard, throwing him sideways.

The knife skittered out of Vale's hands.

Duncan made a grab for it, but Vale got it first and slashed up and around, slicing Duncan's arm.

He swore and stumbled back, a fresh wave of dizziness making him stagger.

Vale stumbled, too, struggling to maintain his balance.

Duncan quickly backed up, then slammed against a tree behind him.

Vale grinned, victory in his eyes.

"Duncan! Catch!"

Duncan whipped his head around at the sound of Remi's voice. He automatically reached up for what she'd thrown, some kind of club. He caught it and whirled around, swinging it at Vale's head as his assailant swung his arm down toward Duncan's chest.

The club caught Vale in the temple. The knife glanced off Duncan's chest and flew harmlessly through the air. Vale's eyes rolled up and he fell to the ground, unmoving.

Duncan stood unsteady on his feet, his hands fisted as he waited for Vale to get up. He didn't. The side of his head where Duncan had hit him was soaked with blood. The club he'd used appeared to somehow be connected to his head. Something metallic was sticking out, some kind of long pin.

"Duncan, are you okay? Duncan?"

The sound of Remi's footsteps had him turning just in time to catch her in his arms. He clasped her to him, breathing in her scent, his face buried in her hair.

"Remi. Thank God. Remi."

"You're bleeding." She pushed out of his arms,

her eyes wide with fear as she looked at his side. "He stabbed you."

"No. Billy did."

She blinked. "Billy?"

He pulled her against him again. "I'm fine. Don't worry about me. Now that I know you're safe, I'm fine. Thank God you're okay."

She put her arms around him, hugging him back.

The sound of running feet had both of them turning. Lee and four rangers burst from the cover of trees, guns raised.

"Hold up," Duncan called out. "We're okay. Vale is down."

As the men rushed around them, checking on Vale, Duncan slowly lowered himself to the ground. But he didn't release Remi. He held on to her, unable to let her go.

"Duncan, your side. We need to bandage it. And, oh no, your arm. It's bleeding, too!" She pressed her hand against his chest, her eyes filled with anguish and concern.

He feathered his fingers through her hair, unable to stop smiling. "You're okay. Please tell me you're okay."

She smiled. "I'm okay."

"Duncan," Lee called out. "Where the heck did you get this bone? The thing has a long pin in it."

"Bone?" He looked toward Vale and the rangers,

then back at Remi. "What exactly did you toss to me when I was fighting Vale?"

"A miracle. From Becca to me to you. She saved us, Duncan. Becca saved us both."

Chapter Eighteen

The sun was just coming up, casting a warm glow over Remi's beloved Rockies in the distance. She clutched a spray of early spring flowers in her hand as she stared out over the rows of headstones that seemed to stretch to the horizon. In the past, her trips to this cemetery had always made her sad, knowing that Becca's small stone beside their mother's and father's was simply a placeholder, that Becca was still missing and might never be laid to rest with her family.

But she had been found.

And she'd been laid to rest almost a month earlier. As Remi walked the path between graves toward where Becca's new marker had been set, the tears in her eyes weren't tears of grief as they'd been in the past. Instead, they were tears of gratitude. Becca was finally at rest, beside her loving parents, who would watch over her for all eternity.

Although Remi would never know exactly what happened to her sister, it no longer mattered like it once had. Because it was over. Finally. For all of them.

For the first time in her adult life she felt…free. She could move on, begin anew, have a fresh start without the constant questions casting a dark pall over her life. The drive to search for answers and bring her sister home was over.

So why wasn't she happy?

She knew why. Duncan. She missed him, more than she'd ever expected. They'd been thrust together for such a short time, in a powder keg of stress and danger, and a white-hot attraction that had been so consuming, so…impossible, given the situation, that she hadn't trusted it. As soon as Becca had been found, and after Remi's shoulder was seen to and she knew Duncan was going to recover from his wounds, she'd taken her sister home for a private ceremony and laid her to rest in this cemetery between her parents. And she'd gone on with her life. Or tried to. But moving on was proving to be much more difficult than she'd anticipated.

Duncan.

He'd called her several times after she'd left him at the hospital. But she was too much of a coward to talk to him. She didn't know what to say. Instead, she'd simply texted him that she was okay and left it at that.

How could she start a new life, with or without him, move forward, when she didn't know where she wanted to go, what she wanted to do? At least before, she'd had a goal—find Becca. Now? She was like a ship lost at sea, not knowing where to turn.

Her boss had been willing to keep her on at work. But in retrospect, all his criticisms over the years had been spot-on. She'd taken the job with the FBI only because of Becca. And without the need to search for her anymore, what satisfaction she'd once had there had fizzled. She just didn't have that drive she'd once had. She wanted, needed, something else. She just didn't quite know what that might be.

Thankfully, her father's foresight in having a generous life-insurance policy all those years ago, and her subsequent investment of that money, gave her the cushion she needed while making that decision. She'd resigned her position at the FBI. And now she needed to figure out what to do next.

Shaking her head at her jumbled thoughts, she carefully adjusted the bouquet in her hands. The arrangement of irises, daffodils, pansies and pink roses had been culled from her mother's garden, yet another remnant of the past that Remi hadn't been able to let go of all these years. She'd never even moved out of her parents' house. Now the space felt oddly stifling, like she no longer belonged there. She'd put it up for sale last week. It felt…weird, putting it on the market. But it also felt right. She was going to turn twenty-eight in a few weeks. And it was as if she'd just graduated high school and was trying to figure out what she wanted to be when she grew up.

She really hoped she figured it out before it was time to retire.

Stepping past the last row of headstones before her family's, she stopped, and stared. There were three rectangular gray marble tombstones, each with a marble vase attached to the base. And each vase had fresh flowers in it, red roses. The last time that Remi had been here was after the private memorial service that had consisted of the preacher, herself and a handful of Becca's old high school friends who were still in the area. She hadn't come back because she'd waited for the ground to settle, knowing the headstone couldn't be placed until then.

So who had left the fresh roses?

Kneeling on the ground, she winced, then caught herself with her left hand on her mother's tombstone. The right shoulder was getting much better with therapy. She didn't even wear the sling anymore. But it still reminded her on occasion that the injury was there, with a fresh rush of pain that zapped her like a jolt of electricity. She rubbed her shoulder, then picked up the flowers she'd brought and arranged them around the roses.

After finishing with the vases on both her parents' graves, she moved to the last one, Becca's. That's when she saw the piece of paper folded up and perched between two of the roses. She carefully pulled it out and unfolded it. Her hands shook as she recognized the handwriting. It was the same as what she'd seen on another note, sitting on a nightstand, on a cold February night, a lifetime ago.

Remi, I hope that with Easter coming up in a few days, the time of fresh starts and new beginnings, that you, too, are able to get that fresh start that you wanted. It is my fervent wish that you be at peace and that you're happy. But no matter what, you'll never be alone. I'm there with you, in thought, in spirit. Always. All my love, Duncan.

A drop of moisture plopped onto the paper, making the ink bleed. She glanced up at the sky, expecting to see rain clouds. But it wasn't raining. She was crying. She wiped her eyes, let out a shaky breath and looked down at the note.

"All my love, Duncan."

"All my love."

"Love." Was that an Irish salutation or did it mean that he actually loved her?

"Idiot! Stop wasting time."

She snapped her head up and looked around.

"Get your lazy butt up."

She jerked her head toward the tombstone, and blinked. "Becca? Is that you?"

"Get up!"

She climbed awkwardly to her feet, bracing herself with her left hand, favoring her right shoulder. The voice had been so loud, so…real. Just like when she'd been in the Smokies, lying hurt on the ground, and she'd heard her sister's irritated voice in her ear, telling her to run. She looked around, relieved when she didn't see anyone else close enough to realize she was hearing voices. Then she licked her dry lips. "Becca? Is…is that you? Are you trying to tell me something?"

The wind picked up suddenly, rattling the note in her hand. She looked at it, sad to see that she'd obviously had more than one tear fall on the paper. Her tears had pretty much obliterated the ink. All she could read now was "my love, Duncan."

A gust blew against her, pushing her back several feet, and snatched the note from her hands. She grabbed at it, but it swirled just out of her reach, bouncing across the grass in the direction of the parking lot.

She hesitated, looked at her parents' tombstones, at Becca's.

"Run!"

Remi smiled, fresh tears dripping down her cheeks. "Subtlety never was your strong suit, was it, sis?" She wiped her eyes and looked at the three pieces of stone. And she knew this wasn't where they were. Her family would always be in her heart. She would carry them with her wherever she went. They would never be alone.

And neither would she.

The wind tugged at her hair again. She smiled. "I love you, Mom, Dad. I love you, too, Becca."

A warm gentle breeze, nothing like the raging wind from earlier, picked up the long tendrils of her curly dark hair and settled them softly around her shoulders.

She let out a ragged breath. "Thank you, Becca." She took off running toward her car.

DUNCAN SETTLED THE tray of ham that he'd just sliced in the middle of his parents' enormous dining room table. Adam set the turkey beside it.

"I think that's the last of it," Adam said.

Duncan nodded. As usual, his mother had gone all out. The table was set with her fine china, plus the gold flatware she normally kept in a velvet-lined box in the hutch at the other end of the room. Even the fancy crystal candleholders had been moved from their place of honor on the mantel in the family room to the table, one on each end of a platter of meat. The white candles mixed their vanilla scent with the aroma of an Easter dinner that would see each of them with leftovers for days to come.

The sounds of laughter came through the archway to the kitchen. His father's deep voice rumbled and his mother and Jody laughed in response.

Duncan noted there was an extra chair, as usual.

Adam followed his gaze. "Ever the optimist. When's the last time Ian showed up for a holiday meal?" He shook his head.

"Christmas a year ago," a voice said from the doorway.

They both turned to see Colin step into the dining room from the family room. "But I always show up so you can bask in the presence of the favorite son." He grinned and held out his arms with a flourish, as if bestowing a magnanimous gift on them by simply being there.

Adam and Duncan exchanged a glance and rolled their eyes. "Mom!" they both yelled.

She ducked her head in from the kitchen, wiping her hands on a dish towel. "Inside voices. Were you raised in a barn? I swear I—" She broke off her lecture when she saw Colin, a barely shorter copy of

Duncan and Adam, which made him six-two instead of their six-three.

"Ma. I'm home!" He spread his arms again.

"Colin!" She half turned toward the kitchen. "Colin's here!" She ran to him and he wrapped his arms around her, a big grin on his face as he looked at Duncan and Adam and silently mouthed, *"Favorite."*

"About time," Adam complained. "Now we can eat." He softened his words with a smile and headed in for a group hug.

Duncan laughed and clapped Colin on the shoulder, deftly avoiding the group hug and heading into the family room. As soon as he was out of sight of his family, he stopped smiling. Keeping up pretenses of being happy and acting like his world hadn't been ripped apart was taking its toll. If he got through the rest of this smiling, laughing family day with his sanity intact, it would be a miracle.

He lifted his right boot and rested it on the fireplace hearth as he stared into the flames. It had been about two months since Remi Jordan had blown through his life and left him a wrecked man. He'd known he cared about her. But he hadn't known just how much until he'd nearly lost her to a brutal man's knife. And then, after visiting him in the hospital to make sure he survived his injuries from his encounter with Vale, for her to just…leave, to go back to Colorado without a backward glance… He shook his head. Flying there a few days ago and putting the flowers and that note on her sister's grave had been the act of a lovesick idiot. Obviously she didn't feel the same way he did or she'd have responded to his calls or that foolish note by now. Somehow he was going to have to figure out how to go on with his life with a big gaping hole in his chest where his heart used to be.

He just wished he knew how.

The doorbell rang. He frowned and looked over his shoulder to see if his dad was going to get the door. This was their cabin, after all. And Duncan had zero expectations of his black-sheep youngest brother, Ian, actually showing up. So whoever it was had to be here to see his dad or mom.

It was noisy back in the dining room with the mini–family reunion going on. Colin was in the middle of some kind of secret assignment in his capacity as a U.S. Deputy Marshal. And yet, somehow, he always managed to make it home for holidays. Everyone was obviously too preoccupied to notice the door.

The bell rang again.

Duncan sighed and crossed the expansive family room with its two-story view of the Smokies and opened the door.

He promptly forgot how to breathe.

"Hi, Duncan." Remi gave him a tremulous smile, her brown eyes as warm as honey as she stared up at him. "I hope you don't mind me showing up at your parents' home. I tracked you down through your boss." A light breeze toyed with her dark brown curls, swirling them around her face. She impatiently shoved them back.

"You dyed your hair again." A stupid thing to say,

but it was all his shocked brain could come up with at the moment.

Her smile dimmed. "Yeah, well. It's as close to my natural color as I could get. I'm through with dyeing and changing my hair. I quit my job at the FBI. I'm plain old Remi Jordan again." She waited, her gaze searching his.

He stood frozen to the spot, not sure what to say, what to do. He opened his mouth several times, but couldn't seem to make any more words come out.

"Duncan?" his mother's voice called out from behind him. "Who's there?" She pretty much pushed him out of the way and stepped into the open doorway. Duncan saw her smile falter, probably because she'd hoped it was her youngest son. But she quickly recovered and gave Remi a warm, welcoming smile. "Hello there, young lady. Happy Easter."

Remi smiled back, but her smile was much less bright, her expression more guarded now, unsure as she shook his mother's hand.

"Mrs. McKenzie, right? I'm Remi Jordan. Sorry to crash your Easter celebrations. But I was looking for Duncan and I—"

"Remi Jordan?" His mother's eyes widened in surprise. "Oh, my. The FBI agent who..." She faltered, obviously not wanting to bring up bad memories about Becca and what had happened.

Remi took his mother's hands in hers. "It's okay to say it. The FBI agent who came here looking for her missing sister. And found her. Becca's home now, with my parents, and with God. I'm at peace with it."

His mother pulled her into a hug. "You poor, dear child. Come in, come in. You're just in time for dinner."

Remi's eyes widened as she pulled back. "Oh, no. No, ma'am. I couldn't. I really should have waited, but I was, well, I just really wanted to talk to Duncan. If I could." She looked up at him. "Duncan? Can we talk?"

He cleared his throat and drew a ragged breath. Seeing her again had sucked all the oxygen from his brain and made him dumbstruck. Both his mother and Remi were looking at him with concern, or in his mother's case, as if she thought he'd lost every good manner she'd ever taught him. She looked as if she was ready to twist his ear and drag him inside if he didn't speak.

"Give us a minute" was all he could manage, which he knew he'd pay for later. His mother didn't tolerate rudeness.

He grabbed Remi's left hand and tugged her behind him as he headed around the corner of the house.

Chapter Nineteen

Remi allowed Duncan to tow her around the outside of the cabin, using the opportunity to blink back the stupid tears burning her eyes. She'd never felt so humiliated, so ashamed, in all her life. She'd spent a ridiculous amount of money that she couldn't afford to grab a last-minute flight on a holiday and fly halfway across the country to see him. While she hadn't necessarily expected that he'd get down on one knee and pledge his undying love, she'd assumed he'd at least smile at her, hug her, something to let her know that he was actually glad to see her. Instead, he'd glowered at her and hadn't even bothered to introduce her to his mother before yanking her after him like a dog on a leash.

She should have stayed in Colorado.

Instead, she'd built up that stupid note into a fantasy of happily-ever-after, when it had probably just been a colleague paying his respects to her family and wishing her well. The End. Done. Over. She felt so stupid. And hurt. She was surprised her heart was still beating after the huge crack he'd just made in it.

All she wanted to do was run back to her rental car and hightail it to the airport to nurse her wounded pride and shattered soul.

They'd just turned another corner around the massive log cabin, into what she supposed would have passed as a backyard if the monstrosity wasn't perched on the edge of the mountain, with a network of stilts jammed into the ground, holding the house up. Her earlier belief that Duncan came from money was definitely spot on. Which just pointed out another big difference between the two of them. She really shouldn't have come. What had she been thinking?

He stopped and whirled to face her. She automatically retreated from the intensity of his gaze and jerked to a halt when the wall of logs pressed against her back.

"Why are you here?" he demanded.

Her face flushed with heat. "Nice to see you, too."

"Remi. You can't expect to just show up out of the blue and—"

"Assume you'd be happy to see me? Let's not belabor that point. I get it. Loud and clear. You're not happy to see me. And this was a huge, ginormous, not to mention expensive, mistake." She stepped to the side to get around him.

He blocked her in, forcing her against the house again. She fisted her hands at her sides and glared up at him. "Okay, this bully thing ends right here. Back off. Now. Before I kick the family jewels into the back of your throat."

His brows rose, then he blinked and did as she'd

said, giving her some breathing room. He stared at her, swore, cleared his throat.

"Not much for talking today, I see," she said. "No problem. I think we're done here. Really done this time. Have a great holiday with the family. I won't be bothering you again." She turned to stalk off and could have sworn he growled at her. But before she could even glance his way, he grabbed her.

With one arm around her hips, the other at her back, he whirled her around and slammed his mouth down on top of hers. She was so startled she didn't have the presence of mind to kick him as she'd warned. But then his mouth and tongue obliterated her capability of thought, and all she could do was hold on and enjoy the ride.

His big, hot, hard body surrounded hers, cocooning her against the house. His kiss tasted of desperation and anger and heat, all at the same time. But there was something else, too, something she couldn't quite define. She was out of breath and gasping for air when he broke the kiss. His shoulders were heaving as he, too, drew ragged breaths. And then his gaze met hers, and the pain in the deep blue depths had her gasping with surprise.

"Why are you here?" he demanded again, sounding more bewildered and resentful than angry this time.

She'd hurt him. Badly. And she hadn't even realized it until this very moment. The proof was staring back at her. The heat was there between them. It always had been. But the emotions rolling off him in waves had nothing to do with lust and everything to do with a man who'd cared about someone, who still cared about her, and was afraid to hope.

Her anger evaporated. Her body relaxed. She smiled and feathered her hands up his chest.

He jerked at her touch. But he didn't move away.

"Thank you for the flowers you sent to my family. I saw the note."

He frowned. "You could have thanked me over the phone."

She hesitated, still feeling like a fool. But she'd gone to a lot of trouble to get here and she wasn't leaving until she told him what she'd come to say. If he didn't want her after that, so be it. She'd go home, lick her wounds and live her life without him.

Somehow.

After drawing a deep breath, she said, "I'm not here to thank you. I'm here to tell you something that I should have told you a long time ago."

His look turned stony, and this time he did step back, forcing her to drop her arms. "Whatever it is, I'm sure you could have used the phone for that, too. My family's probably waiting dinner on me. I'll walk you to your car."

"I love you."

He jerked his head toward her. His throat worked, his Adam's apple bobbing in his throat. "What did you say?"

Determined to give this everything she had, she stepped toward him and then hooked her hands in his belt loops so that if he moved away again, he'd take her with him. "I'm sorry, Duncan. I'm sorry that I left. But as someone I know once told me, if I had it to do all over again, I still would have left. It was something I had to do. I had to take Becca home and lay the past to rest and work some things out in my mind. You have to understand. All my adult life has been geared toward one thing, one goal—find Becca. Once I did that, once we did that, it was like I was floating in space and someone cut my lifeline. I was lost, struggling, didn't know what to do. Nothing felt right or real. I had to sort it all out, find my center again."

"You said goodbye in the hospital, then walked away. I didn't know you were leaving for good. You didn't answer my calls. All you did was text me that you were okay. I deserved better than that."

Her heart squeezed in her chest at the pain in his words. "I know. You did. You do. That was wrong of me, so very wrong. It's no excuse, but I was confused. The words that I wanted to say were right there, on the tip of my tongue, but I couldn't make sense of them. You and me, we don't make sense." She waved at the expensive home and land. "We really, really don't make sense."

She drew a shaky breath and focused on what she was trying to tell him. And hoped it would be enough. "I was worried that it wasn't real, the way I feel about you. How could it be after knowing you for such a short period of time? I wasn't ready for that, for you. There wasn't room in my confused mind to understand it, let alone face it. So, yes. I walked away. But

I'm here now. I came back. I came back for you, Duncan. I wasn't ready before. But now I am."

He searched her eyes, then took a step. Toward her. "What are you saying, Remi? What are you ready for?"

"You. I'm ready for you. I love you, Duncan. I want everything you said in the note you sent me. I want a fresh start, a new beginning. I want to be happy. And there's only one thing that will make me happy. You. Always and forever."

He shuddered and reached for her. He didn't kiss her this time. Instead, he wrapped his arms around her, pulling her tightly against him.

"I thought I'd lost you," he said. "I thought I'd lost you."

She wrapped her arms around his waist. "I'm right here."

He drew back and cupped her face. "For how long?"

She blinked, not sure what he meant. "As long as you want me? If you want me, that is. I put my parents' house up for sale. I packed all my clothes, and I do mean all of them. I have four massive suitcases in my rental car. Cost me a fortune at the airport to check those bags."

"Where are you staying?"

He wasn't giving her many clues about how he felt. Her face heated as she put her pride, and her heart, on the line. "With you? I hope. That is, if your cabin's been repaired from the shoot-out and you want me there."

His eyes widened. "If I want you? Seriously?" He

reached into his shirt and pulled out a chain that was hanging around his neck, then held it up. A diamond solitaire ring glittered in the sunlight.

"Is that?" She had to clear her tight throat. "Is that what I think it is?" Her voice was hoarse and raw.

He undid the chain and pulled off the ring, letting the chain drop to the ground. He got down on one knee in front of her and held up the ring.

"Remi Elizabeth Jordan—"

"How did you know my middle name?"

He arched a brow. "I'm a criminal investigator."

She smiled.

He grinned. "Remi, I love that sassy mouth of yours, your sexy little body, that gorgeous complicated brain inside your pretty little head. I love everything about you. But mostly I love the idea of having you as my wife, to have and to hold, for better or worse, until death do us part."

Unshed tears clogged her throat. "Shouldn't we save the vows for when we're in front of the preacher?"

"Is that a yes?"

"I don't remember you asking me a question," she teased.

"Nothing's ever easy with you is it, sweet Colleen?"

"Now where would the fun be in that, Irish lad?" She smiled at him through the tears that she could no longer hold back.

"Marry me?" His voice was so full of love and tenderness that she nearly melted into a puddle at his feet.

Unable to speak, she held her left hand out. It shook so hard he finally had to hold it still so he could get the ring on her finger.

Then he was kissing her, searing her with his heat. And she was kissing him back, trying to show him with actions how much she adored this smart, sexy, wonderful man.

When he finally broke the kiss, a chorus of catcalls and whistles rang out from above. They both looked up. Five happy faces looked down at them, leaning over the balcony railing.

Heat flushed Remi's face as she returned their waves.

Duncan laughed and swooped in for another kiss, much to the amusement of their audience. He pulled back, feathered her face with more kisses as if he couldn't get enough of her. His expression turned serious.

"I love you, Remi."

"I love you, Duncan. More than you'll ever know."

He cupped her face in his hands and stared down at her, his brow furrowed with concern. "You won't ever be alone again. You'll always have your family, the memories, their love in your heart. But you'll have me now, too. And a new family who will learn to love you almost as much as I do, if you want that. But they can be…intense. A lot to deal with. If you need more time, we don't have to stay here today. We can go to my cabin and—"

She put her finger on his lips to stop him. "And

miss that mouthwatering dinner I smelled at the front door? Not a chance."

His mouth curved into a sexy grin that had her regretting her offer to stay. Having him at his cabin, all to herself, was more mouthwatering than any food could ever be.

He gently wiped the tears from her cheeks and tucked her arm in the crook of his elbow. "Come on, future wife. I'll introduce you to your new family."

He kissed her again, a sweet, soft, tender kiss that healed the large crack from earlier, encasing her heart in the warmth and strength of his love. And then he took her to the front of the house, where her new family was waiting to welcome her with open arms.

* * * * *

Look for more books in award-winning author Lena Diaz's The Mighty McKenzies miniseries, coming soon.

And don't miss the previous title in the series:

Smoky Mountains Ranger

Available now from Harlequin Intrigue!

Get 4 FREE REWARDS!

We'll send you 2 FREE Books
plus 2 FREE Mystery Gifts.

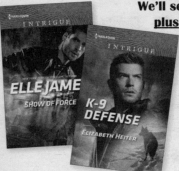

Harlequin Intrigue® books feature heroes and heroines that confront and survive danger while finding themselves irresistibly drawn to one another.

FREE
Value Over
$20

YES! Please send me 2 FREE Harlequin Intrigue® novels and my 2 FREE gifts (gifts are worth about $10 retail). After receiving them, if I don't wish to receive any more books, I can return the shipping statement marked "cancel." If I don't cancel, I will receive 6 brand-new novels every month and be billed just $4.99 each for the regular-print edition or $5.74 each for the larger-print edition in the U.S., or $5.74 each for the regular-print edition or $6.49 each for the larger-print edition in Canada. That's a savings of at least 12% off the cover price! It's quite a bargain! Shipping and handling is just 50¢ per book in the U.S. and 75¢ per book in Canada.* I understand that accepting the 2 free books and gifts places me under no obligation to buy anything. I can always return a shipment and cancel at any time. The free books and gifts are mine to keep no matter what I decide.

Choose one: ☐ **Harlequin Intrigue®**
Regular-Print
(182/382 HDN GMYW)

☐ **Harlequin Intrigue®**
Larger-Print
(199/399 HDN GMYW)

Name (please print)

Address   Apt. #

City   State/Province   Zip/Postal Code

Mail to the Reader Service:
IN U.S.A.: P.O. Box 1341, Buffalo, NY 14240-8531
IN CANADA: P.O. Box 603, Fort Erie, Ontario L2A 5X3

Want to try 2 free books from another series! Call 1-800-873-8635 or visit www.ReaderService.com.

---

*Terms and prices subject to change without notice. Prices do not include sales taxes, which will be charged (if applicable) based on your state or country of residence. Canadian residents will be charged applicable taxes. Offer not valid in Quebec. This offer is limited to one order per household. Books received may not be as shown. Not valid for current subscribers to Harlequin Intrigue books. All orders subject to approval. Credit or debit balances in a customer's account(s) may be offset by any other outstanding balance owed by or to the customer. Please allow 4 to 6 weeks for delivery. Offer available while quantities last.

Your Privacy—The Reader Service is committed to protecting your privacy. Our Privacy Policy is available online at www.ReaderService.com or upon request from the Reader Service. We make a portion of our mailing list available to reputable third parties that offer products we believe may interest you. If you prefer that we not exchange your name with third parties, or if you wish to clarify or modify your communication preferences, please visit us at www.ReaderService.com/consumerschoice or write to us at Reader Service Preference Service, P.O. Box 9062, Buffalo, NY 14240-9062. Include your complete name and address.

HI19R2

SPECIAL EXCERPT FROM

⊞ HARLEQUIN®

I N T R I G U E

*Jen Delaney and Ty Carson were once sweethearts, but
that's in the past. When Ty starts receiving threatening
letters that focus more and more on Jen, he'll do
whatever it takes to keep her safe—even kidnap her.*

Read on for a sneak preview of
Wyoming Cowboy Ranger *by Nicole Helm.*

Jen Delaney loved Bent, Wyoming, the town she'd been born in,
grown up in. She was a respected member of the community, in
part because she ran the only store that sold groceries and other
essentials within a twenty-mile radius of town.

From her position crouched on the linoleum while she stocked
shelves, she looked around the small store she'd taken over at the
ripe age of eighteen. For the past ten years it had been her baby,
with its narrow aisles and hodgepodge of necessities.

She'd always known she'd spend the entirety of her life happily
ensconced in Bent and her store, no matter what happened around
her.

The reappearance of Ty Carson didn't change that knowledge
so much as make it...annoying. No, annoying would have been
just his being in town again. The fact their families had somehow
intermingled in the last year was...a catastrophe.

Her sister, Laurel, marrying Ty's cousin Grady had been a shock,
very close to a betrayal, though it was hard to hold it against Laurel
when Grady was so head over heels for her it was comical. They
both glowed with love and happiness and impending parenthood.

Jen tried not to hate them for it.

She could forgive Cam, her eldest brother, for his serious
relationship with Hilly. Hilly was biologically a Carson, but she'd
only just found that out. Besides, Hilly wasn't like other Carsons.
She was so sweet and earnest.

But Dylan and Vanessa… Her business-minded, sophisticated older brother *impregnating* and marrying snarky bad girl Vanessa Carson… *That* was a nightmare.

And none of it was fair. Jen was now, out of nowhere, surrounded by Carsons and Delaneys intermingling—which went against everything Bent had ever stood for. Carsons and Delaneys hated each other. They didn't fall in love and get married and have *babies*.

And still, she could have handled all that in a certain amount of stride if it weren't for *Ty* Carson. Everywhere she turned he seemed to be right there, his stoic gaze always locked on *her*, reminding her of a past she'd spent a lot of time trying to bury and forget.

When she'd been seventeen and the stupidest girl alive, she would have done anything for Ty Carson. Risked the Delaney-Carson curse that, even with all these Carson-Delaney marriages, Bent still had their heart set on. She would have risked her father's wrath over daring to connect herself with a *Carson*. She would have given up anything and everything for Ty.

Instead he'd made promises to love her forever, then disappeared to join the army—which she'd found out only a good month after the fact. He hadn't just broken her heart—he'd crushed it to bits.

But Ty was a blip of her past she'd been able to forget about, mostly, for the past ten years. She'd accepted his choices and moved on with her life. For a decade she had grown into the adult who didn't care at all about Ty Carson.

Then Ty had come home for good, and all she'd convinced herself of faded away.

She was half convinced he'd returned simply to make her miserable.

"You look angry. Must be thinking about me."

Don't miss
Wyoming Cowboy Ranger *by Nicole Helm,*
available June 2019 wherever
Harlequin® Intrigue books and ebooks are sold.

www.Harlequin.com

HIEXP0519

*Dr. Rowan DuPont has returned to Winchester,
Tennessee, to take over the family funeral home, but
she is haunted by the memories of her family members'
murders. Rowan is prepared to face her past in order
to do right by her father's wishes...and to wait out his
murderer, a serial killer who is obsessed with her.*

Read on for a sneak preview of
The Secrets We Bury
by USA TODAY *bestselling author Debra Webb.*

Winchester, Tennessee
Monday, May 6, 7:15 a.m.

Mothers shouldn't die this close to Mother's Day.

Especially mothers whose daughters, despite being
grown and having families of their own, still considered
Mom to be their best friend. Rowan DuPont had spent
the better part of last night consoling the daughters of
Geneva Phillips. Geneva had failed to show at church
on Sunday morning, and later that same afternoon she
wasn't answering her cell. Her younger daughter entered
her mother's home to check on her and found Geneva
deceased in the bathtub.

Now the seventy-two-year-old woman's body waited
in refrigeration for Rowan to begin the preparations for
her final journey. The viewing wasn't until tomorrow
evening, so there was no particular rush. The husband

of one of the daughters was away on business in London and wouldn't arrive back home until late today. There was time for a short break, which turned into a morning drive that had taken Rowan across town and to a place she hadn't visited in more than two decades.

Like death, some things were inevitable. Coming back to this place was one of those things. Perhaps it was the hours spent with the sisters last night that had prompted memories of Rowan's own sister. She and her twin had once been inseparable. Wasn't that generally the way with identical twins?

The breeze shifted, lifting a wisp of hair across her face. Rowan swiped it away and stared out over Tims Ford Lake. The dark, murky waters spread like sprawling arms some thirty-odd miles upstream from the nearby dam, enveloping the treacherous Elk River in its embrace. The water was deep and unforgiving. Even standing on the bank, at least ten feet from the edge, a chill crept up Rowan's spine. She hated this place. Hated the water. The ripples that broke the shadowy surface…the smell of fish and rotting plant life. She hated every little thing about it.

This was the spot where her sister's body had been found.

Don't miss
The Secrets We Bury *by Debra Webb,*
available May 2019 wherever
MIRA® *books and ebooks are sold.*

www.Harlequin.com